Diana wanted to take another peek

at the construction worker outside her kitchen window. He was a big man, brawny and tan, with coal-black hair some might think needed a trim.

She didn't think so. Hair that was a bit long and unruly looked good on him. And he had one of those don't-mess-with-me auras. Something that suggested he hadn't been pampered.

It had been a long time since a guy with an edge had turned her head. But Diana knew better than to get involved with anyone again. Just the other night, while tucking her daughters into bed and listening to their prayers, her daughters had asked God for a new daddy to make their family complete. But Diana hadn't been able to utter an amen to that.

She didn't want another husband. Every man who'd ever loved her, every man she should have been able to depend upon, had disappointed her or hurt her, in one way or another.

Yet, for some silly reason, she couldn't help looking out the kitchen window one last time.

Dear Reader,

June, the ideal month for weddings, is the perfect time to celebrate true love. And we are doing it in style here at Silhouette Special Edition as we celebrate the conclusion of several wonderful series. With *For the Love of Pete*, Sherryl Woods happily marries off the last of her ROSE COTTAGE SISTERS. It's Jo's turn this time—and she'd thought she'd gotten Pete Catlett out of her system for good. But at her childhood haven, anything can happen! Next, MONTANA MAVERICKS: GOLD RUSH GROOMS concludes with Cheryl St.John's *Million-Dollar Makeover*. We finally learn the identity of the true heir to the Queen of Hearts Mine—and no one is more shocked than the owner herself, the plain-Jane town… dog walker. When she finds herself in need of financial advice, she consults devastatingly handsome Riley Douglas—but she soon finds his influence exceeds the business sphere.…

And speaking of conclusions, Judy Duarte finishes off her BAYSIDE BACHELORS miniseries with *The Matchmakers' Daddy*, in which a wrongly imprisoned ex-con finds all kinds of second chances with a beautiful single mother and her adorable little girls. Next up in GOING HOME, Christine Flynn's heartwarming miniseries, is *The Sugar House*, in which a man who comes home to right a wrong finds himself falling for the woman who's always seen him as her adversary. Patricia McLinn's next book in her SOMETHING OLD, SOMETHING NEW… miniseries, *Baby Blues and Wedding Bells*, tells the story of a man who suddenly learns that his niece is really…his daughter. And in *The Secrets Between Them* by Nikki Benjamin, a divorced woman who's falling hard for her gardener learns that he is in reality an investigator hired by her ex-father-in-law to try to prove her an unfit mother.

So enjoy all those beautiful weddings, and be sure to come back next month! Here's hoping you catch the bouquet.…

Gail Chasan
Senior Editor

Please address questions and book requests to:
Silhouette Reader Service
U.S.: 3010 Walden Ave., P.O. Box 1325, Buffalo, NY 14269
Canadian: P.O. Box 609, Fort Erie, Ont. L2A 5X3

THE MATCHMAKERS' DADDY

JUDY DUARTE

SPECIAL EDITION®

Published by Silhouette Books

America's Publisher of Contemporary Romance

To Betty Astleford,
who never met a bad boy she didn't like. You've taught
us a lot about tolerance and second chances.

I love you, Mom.

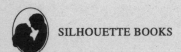 SILHOUETTE BOOKS

ISBN 0-373-24689-7

THE MATCHMAKERS' DADDY

Copyright © 2005 by Judy Duarte

All rights reserved. Except for use in any review, the reproduction
or utilization of this work in whole or in part in any form by any
electronic, mechanical or other means, now known or hereafter
invented, including xerography, photocopying and recording, or in
any information storage or retrieval system, is forbidden without
the written permission of the editorial office, Silhouette Books,
233 Broadway, New York, NY 10279 U.S.A.

All characters in this book have no existence outside the imagination of
the author and have no relation whatsoever to anyone bearing the same
name or names. They are not even distantly inspired by any individual
known or unknown to the author, and all incidents are pure invention.

This edition published by arrangement with Harlequin Books S.A.

® and TM are trademarks of Harlequin Books S.A., used under license.
Trademarks indicated with ® are registered in the United States Patent
and Trademark Office, the Canadian Trade Marks Office and in other
countries.

Visit Silhouette Books at www.eHarlequin.com

Printed in U.S.A.

JUDY DUARTE

An avid reader who enjoys a happy ending, Judy Duarte always wanted to write books of her own. One day, she decided to make that dream come true. Five years and six manuscripts later, she sold her first book to Silhouette Special Edition.

Her unpublished stories have won the Emily and the Orange Rose, and in 2001, she became a double Golden Heart finalist. Judy credits her success to Romance Writers of America and two wonderful critique partners, Sheri WhiteFeather and Crystal Green, both of whom write for Silhouette.

At times, when a stubborn hero and a headstrong heroine claim her undivided attention, she and her family are thankful for fast food, pizza delivery and video games. When she's not at the keyboard or in a Walter Mitty–type world, she enjoys traveling, spending romantic evenings with her personal hero and playing board games with her kids.

Judy lives in Southern California and loves to hear from her readers. You may write to her at: P.O. Box 498, San Luis Rey, CA 92068-0498. You can also visit her Web site at www.judyduarte.com.

From the *Bayside Banner*:

Two men, one armed with a 9mm automatic, robbed the Speedy-Stop on Richland Road last night. Shots rang out as Charles Tompkins, owner of the convenience store, tried to defend himself and his clerk, Clara Willet, a forty-seven-year-old grandmother of two.

The gunman ran off with an estimated four hundred dollars, but his accomplice, nineteen-year-old Zachary Henderson, was arrested at the scene.

Marilyn Santos, who lives down the street from the Speedy-Stop and was in the store at the time, said, "That Zack Henderson has been a juvenile delinquent for years and is a known troublemaker. He said he wasn't involved in the robbery, but I saw him and the other man get out of the same car and enter the store together."

Mrs. Willet was shot in the shoulder and is being treated at Oceana General Hospital. The condition of Mr. Tompkins, who received a gunshot wound to the back, was not available at press time.

Chapter One

Zack Henderson was used to neighborhood kids gawking at him when he ran the bulldozer at local construction sites, but usually those kids were boys.

What possible interest could girls have in tractors, dirt and diesel fuel?

Along the block wall that separated the backyards of an older neighborhood from the future site of a new subdivision, two little girls perched in the summer sun, giggling, whispering to themselves and occasionally waving at him.

And for some goofy reason, he would always wave back. Maybe because it made him feel a bit heroic, in spite of being anything but.

He wiped his hand across his forehead, drying the perspiration that gathered there. Then he took a swig of water from the jug he kept in the cab of his dozer.

God, it was hot today. He glanced at the girls and wondered when they'd get tired or bored and go inside. Not anytime soon, he guessed. The heat and noise didn't seem to bother them at all.

They were cute kids. The smaller one had brown, curly, shoulder-length hair and held a teddy bear in the crook of her arm.

The older girl, a blonde with long hair, looked about ten or eleven. While Zack watched, she took a drink from the red plastic cup that rested between them, then wiggled her fingers at him again. And like he'd done several times over the course of the afternoon, he smiled and waved back.

Their interest in him and his tractor had him stumped. But what did an ex-con like him know about kids—especially girls?

He'd only met Emily, his four-year-old daughter, for the very first time a couple of months ago, just after he'd been paroled. And he still felt way out of his league. But he *had* learned Emily was big on kitties and new party shoes—not bulldozers, dust and noise.

The warm, pungent smell of diesel and the roar of the engine hung in the cab of the D9L Caterpillar, as Zack continued to clear and grub the thirty-seven acres that would soon be a new housing development called Mariposa Glen.

Bob Adams, the owner of Bayside Construction, had taken a chance and hired Zack right out of prison, going so far as to write letters to the parole board on his behalf and getting him into the union. Bob used to live down the street from Zack and his uncle, and when Zack started working on an old beat-up truck in the driveway, Bob would stop by and shoot the breeze about the Chargers, rebuilt engines and stuff like that.

At the time, Zack hadn't thought of Bob as a friend, since there was a fifteen- to-twenty-year age difference between them. But the older man's faith in him had been one of the first breaks Zack had received since his conviction.

And it wasn't something he'd ever forget.

Zack swiped at his brow again. After lunch—about the time the girls had taken an interest in his work—he'd shed his shirt. But the heat of the summer sun hadn't eased up much, even though it was nearing five and he'd been on overtime for an hour or so.

As he turned the dozer, he again looked at the wall where the children sat. The blonde lifted the hand that rested near her beverage, but before he could nod or acknowledge her, the little brown-haired girl reached to take a drink while juggling her teddy bear. The stuffed animal slipped from her grasp, and as she tried to catch it, she lost her balance and tumbled forward.

Damn. That was a long, hard fall for a little kid.

He quickly decelerated, threw the gear into Neutral, lowered the dozer blade, then jumped from the rig and ran toward the crying child, who lay on the ground in a heap of pink and white.

His heart echoed in his chest, as he leaped over clods of dirt and twigs that had yet to be cleared.

The older girl tried to scramble off the wall, but was having a difficult time of it.

When he reached the child in the dirt, he knelt by her side. "Are you all right?"

"No," she shrieked between sobs. "I broke my leg. And my back. And my bottom. And it hurts *really* bad."

The crazy kid could have broken her neck. As she sat up and peered at her knee, which sported a blood-tinged scrape, she let out a piercing wail.

"I'll go get Mommy's doctor book," the older girl said, as she turned and tried to figure out how to scale the six-foot wall.

"Why don't you go get your mommy instead," Zack suggested. He could use some backup. Surely the child's mother could handle this situation a hell of a lot better than he could. For Pete's sake, he'd never felt so inept in all his life.

"Our mom is at work," the older girl said.

"And what about your dad?" he asked her.

"He's in Heaven."

Oops. What was he supposed to say to that?

Hoping to distract the crying child from her pain

and get her thoughts off the loss of her father, he asked her name.

She sniffled, sucking back her tears in a ragged wheeze. "J-Jessie."

"It's Jessica Marie," the older girl supplied. "My name is Becky. I was named after my grandmother, Rebecca Ann. She's in Heaven, too."

Zack didn't want to touch the Heaven stuff with a ten-foot pole, so he clamped his mouth shut.

"What's *your* name?" Becky asked.

He really didn't want to get chummy with a couple of kids. But he didn't want to be rude, either. "You can call me Zack." He didn't give her a last name; he didn't see a point.

"Our mom's name is Diana," she added. "She's very pretty. And she's nice, too."

He knew for a fact that some pretty mothers left their children alone. But he didn't think *nice* ones would. "Who's looking after you?"

"Megan," Becky supplied. "Our baby-sitter. She's a teenager."

Thank goodness there was someone better qualified for this than him, even if his successor was in her teens.

The injured child—Jessie—had finally stopped crying, but the tears had left a telltale muddy path along her cheeks.

"Do you think you can stand up?" he asked her.

She shrugged. "I don't know. But I'll try."

"Good. I'll help you. Then we can go find Megan."

As he tried to pull the little girl to her feet, she cried out. "Owie. I can't. My leg is still broken."

It looked okay to him. Just a little red near the knee.

Oh, what the hell. He'd just have to carry her home. The crew was spread a little thin this week, so he was the only one working on this project until Monday. He glanced at the dozer that sat idling in the field. With the blade down, it was safe to leave it for a little while, but he went back to the tractor and turned off the ignition.

When he returned to the girls, he picked up the teddy bear and handed it to Becky, then scooped Jessie into his arms.

"You sure are strong," Becky said, as she walked along beside him.

He shrugged. Jessie didn't weigh much more than his daughter, but he figured Becky was actually referring to his size.

At six foot six and with the bulk he'd built up in the prison gym, Zack got plenty of notice on the street. And not just from kids.

"Your muscles are really big," the smaller girl said. "Just like the 'credible Hulk. Do you get green and big when you get mad?"

A smile tugged at his lips. "I get a little red in the face and puff out my chest. But I pretty much stay this color and size."

They walked along the block wall until they

reached the end, then cut through an unfenced back-yard to the street.

"Which house is yours?" he asked, eager to pass the baton—or rather the child—to the sitter.

Becky pointed ahead. "Our house is the white one with the yellow sunflower on the mailbox. My mom painted it. She's a good artist."

As Zack continued down the street in the direction Becky had indicated, she asked, "Are you married?"

It seemed like an odd question, but he answered truthfully. "No, I'm not."

"That's good."

Uh-oh. Warning bells went off in Zack's head. Surely the preteen didn't have a crush on him. How was a guy supposed to deal with stuff like that?

"Our mom's not married, either," Becky added.

Their mom? Oh, the widow.

He wasn't sure how that came up. But good. Maybe the childish crush thing was the wrong assumption.

"What about you?" he countered. "Are either of you married?"

They both giggled.

Jessie, who no longer appeared to be shaken by her fall, brightened and her brown eyes sparkled. "No, silly. We're just kids."

As Becky lagged behind, Zack turned and noticed she was struggling to keep up with his stride, so he slowed down. He had to do that when walking with Emily, too.

When the girl finally caught up to him, she asked, "Do tractor drivers make a lot of money?"

What kind of question was that? He was making union scale—a damn good wage, especially for a felon. And he'd be able to buy his own house someday. A place with a second bedroom he could fix up for his daughter and a backyard big enough to hold a swing set, a playhouse and all the other outdoor, childhood necessities he'd yet to learn about.

"I'm happy with my paycheck," he told the girl.

"That's good."

He snuck a glance at Becky's bright-eyed, freckled face and saw the wheels turning. For the life of him, he couldn't figure out the direction of her thoughts.

But maybe it was only his imagination. He'd never quite gotten a handle on the complex way women thought. So what made him think a preteen girl would be any simpler?

As they neared the children's house, one side of a duplex, a plump, gray-haired woman stepped onto the porch shared by both families. She frowned and strode toward him, her stubby arms swinging, her chest heaving with exertion. She furrowed her brow and, as she drew near, pointed a finger at him. "What do you think you're doing? You put that child down immediately, or I'll call the police."

Just the thought of the woman calling the cops made Zack's blood run hot and cold. He'd kept his nose clean since a few months before the robbery at the Speedy Stop. But no one in the D.A.'s office had believed his story. After all, he'd been a known juvenile delinquent who'd admitted arriving at the convenience store with the robber and gunman.

So what made him think things would be different now that the teenage troublemaker was a grown-up ex-con?

"He can't put me down," Jessie told the neighbor. "I broke my leg and my back. And he's taking me home."

"She fell off the block wall and onto the construction site," Zack explained, not sure if it would diffuse the older woman's suspicion. "I don't think she's really hurt."

Jessie pooched out her bottom lip. "I am so. I'm hurt *really* bad."

The woman waddled down her steps and met Zack in the street. "You can bring her into my house. I'll take over from here."

That was fine with Zack. He needed to get back on that dozer, since he was working overtime this week and still had another couple of hours before dark. If Bob came out to check on him, Zack wanted the man to see him hard at work and doing a good job.

"Oh, look!" The child in his arms pointed to an old green Plymouth rumbling down the street. "Mommy's home."

At this point, Zack didn't care who took over for

him. He was completely out of his element when it came to looking after wounded kids, even if their injuries were as minor as Jessie's appeared to be.

The Plymouth stopped in the middle of the street, and a slender brunette climbed from the idling car. "What's going on? Jessie, what's the matter?"

"I broke my leg," the girl began, reciting the list of injuries she'd self-diagnosed.

"And this is Zack," her older sister said. "He was driving a tractor in the field and saved her life. Isn't he nice?"

"Yeah," Jessie said. "And Mommy, he's super-strong, too. You should feel his muscles."

Jessie's mother flushed and tucked a strand of honey-brown hair behind her ear. She flashed Zack an appreciative smile. "Thank you for helping my daughter. But I'm not sure what she was doing out in the field, since the girls aren't allowed out of the yard while I'm gone."

"We *weren't* in the field," Becky explained. "We were sitting on the wall, watching Zack work. Then Jessie fell over like Humpty Dumpty."

"And Zack put me together again." Jessie patted him on the shoulder.

A bare shoulder, he realized. But heck, he hadn't had time to think about putting on a shirt. Or cleaning up so that he could make a good impression on a woman who seemed to grow lovelier by the minute.

She blessed Zack with another sweet smile, and his heart skipped a beat.

"Thank you for rescuing Jessie," she told him, before addressing her oldest daughter with a furrowed brow. "Becky, where's Megan?"

"She's sick with a major headache and taking a nap on the sofa. But don't worry. I took good care of Jessie."

Zack couldn't help but arch a brow at that comment, but he supposed she *had* tried to look after her sister—after the fall.

"We'll talk about that later," the mother said.

"Do you want me to carry her inside for you?" Zack asked, surprised that he'd uttered the words. But as crazy as it seemed, he almost wished she'd say yes.

"Thanks, but I can manage." She lifted her arms to take her daughter from him.

As they shifted the girl from one pair of arms to the other, Zack feared he'd get her light blue blouse or her beige slacks dirty.

"Be careful," he told her. "I'm dusty and sweaty."

"That's all right."

Her hand brushed his several times, making his skin tingle.

"I've got her," she said. "Thanks."

For a moment their gazes locked, and something sweet and gentle drew him to her, threatening to leave him tongue-tied and stammering.

Of course, he couldn't very well stand there gawking at her, especially in front of her daughters and neighbor, so he shook off the mushy feeling. "Well, I'd better go."

Her green eyes glimmered as she nodded, but her gaze never left him. He couldn't help wondering if she found him attractive.

But how stupid was that? She was probably trying to determine his character. And with his luck, her maternal instinct would probably snitch, telling her he'd spent the past five years in prison.

"Thanks again," she said, giving him his cue, his excuse to cut out and return to work.

But he just stood there. "You're welcome."

The unsmiling neighbor stepped closer, eyeing him in a way the girls' mother hadn't. "You look familiar. Have you lived in Bayside long?"

No, he hadn't. But five years ago, his picture had been plastered on the front page of every newspaper in San Diego county, including the *Bayside Banner.* "I moved to town a couple of months ago."

The older woman furrowed her brow, as though not believing him. But hell, he'd told her the truth.

"Thanks again for bringing Jessie home," the girls' mother said.

"Glad I could help." Then Zack turned and strode away, eager to escape the older woman's gaze.

From behind, he could hear the mother tell her girls to stay off the fence. And that she needed to have a talk with Megan.

What had the girls said their mother's name was? Diana?

He supposed it didn't matter. He doubted he'd ever see her or the girls again.

Still, he couldn't help thinking that she was too young to be a widow. His thoughts drifted to her late husband. Dying wasn't anything a man looked forward to, that's for sure. But leaving a wife like her behind would make it a whole lot worse.

He struggled with the urge to turn his head, to take one last look at the woman whose daughter had told the truth when she'd said her mom was pretty and nice.

But he didn't.

Women like that didn't give men like him a second glance.

Diana carried Jessie to the house, but several times she wanted to turn her head and take another peek at the construction worker who was returning to the job site.

He was a big man, brawny and tanned, with coal-black hair some might think needed a trim.

But she didn't think so. Hair that was a bit long and unruly looked good on him. And so did the tattoo that wrapped around his arm.

Zack had what she'd call a hard edge, although compelling blue eyes and a dimpled smile softened it just enough.

She guessed him to be in his midtwenties, yet it

was tough to tell for sure. Still, she figured he was at least five or six years younger than she was—not that it mattered.

"Zack is really handsome," Becky said. "Don't you think so, Mom? And he's nice, too. Kind of like a hero. Did you see his cool tattoo?"

"I saw it," Martha Ashton interjected. "Those flames on his arm reminded me of the hounds of hell."

Diana averted her face and rolled her eyes. It was only a tattoo, for goodness sake, and certainly nothing to use in judging a man's character. He had, after all, brought Jessie home after she'd fallen and gotten hurt.

"Didn't you see that nasty thing?" Martha asked Diana.

How could she not notice the flicker of flames along a bulging biceps? Diana hadn't seen many tattoos up close. Nor had she seen such a big, muscular man without his shirt. Her father was a truck driver, and he was one of the strongest, bulkiest men she'd ever met.

Until today.

"But *did* you see his tattoo, Mom?" Becky asked.

"Yes, I did. It was…interesting. And I think it was nice of him to bring Jessie home."

Martha harrumphed.

Diana always tried to overlook her neighbor's negativity, if she could. Martha had good intentions but could be a bit intrusive. So she slid her a warm smile. "Thanks for seeing about the girls, Martha. I need to get them home and fix dinner."

"I wish I could look out for them while you're working," Martha said. "But with all my volunteer work, I just don't have the time."

"I understand." Diana turned toward the front stoop. "We're getting along just fine. And Megan's doing a good job."

But was Megan *really* doing a good job watching the girls?

The fact that the teenage girl had neglected to call Diana when she became ill didn't sit very well. And that error in judgment reminded Diana how young and inexperienced her childcare provider was.

But she hadn't been able to afford the summer day-camp program the city provided working parents—at least, not for both girls. So she was doing the best she could, under the circumstances.

Of course, she could have remained in Texas, where her father was able to help financially and could occasionally look after the girls. But that wasn't an option. Not if she wanted her daughters to escape the criticism she'd lived with as a child. She wanted them to grow up with their self-esteem intact.

Her father was as tough and strong as those trucks he drove, big rigs that barreled down the interstate and could crush any other vehicle that got in its way.

That didn't mean Diana didn't love him. He was a good man and an even better provider. But living under his thumb, as well as his roof, had become un-bearable. Over the years, he'd criticized her to a fault.

This sauce needs more salt.

There's not enough starch on this shirt.

Who the hell left this damn crayon on the cof-fee table?

Am I the only one who can see that sock on the laundry room floor?

No matter how hard she tried, first as a young girl trying to run the household after her mother left, then as a grown woman returning home with two girls of her own, her best had never been enough.

"I'll talk to you tomorrow," Martha said, as she walked toward her house.

As Diana turned down her own sidewalk, Megan opened the door.

When the teenager spotted Jessie in Diana's arms, her jaw dropped momentarily. "Oh, my gosh. What happened?"

"I fell and broke my leg," Jessie said. "And Zack saved me."

Megan grimaced, as guilt spread over her lightly freckled face. "I'm sorry. I…uh…got sick and dozed off."

And, consequently, no one had been looking after the girls. The drop on the other side of the wall had to be six feet or more. Thank God Jessie hadn't been seriously injured. She could have broken her neck.

Or she could have been run over by a tractor.

Diana blew out a shaky breath, as she struggled with the urge to snap at the fifteen-year-old. To react the way her father would have. To forget that the teenager had nice parents and had come highly recommended. And that it wasn't Megan's fault she'd become ill today.

It was so unfair to look only at the bad and disregard the good.

But that didn't mean Diana would sweep the issue under the rug. "You should have called me at work, Megan. I would have come home early."

"I didn't want to bother you. I thought if I just laid down for a little while I'd be all right."

"Are you feeling better now?"

Megan shrugged. "I guess so."

Diana carried Jessie into the house and placed her on the sofa. "Call me tomorrow. If you're still sick or have a headache, I'll try to work out something else."

"Okay." The teen grabbed her knapsack and headed out the door. "I'm sorry about falling asleep."

"I know." Diana smiled. "But call me next time, okay?"

When Megan had gone and Jessie had decided she was healed of any and all broken bones, Diana went into the kitchen to start dinner.

Sometimes it was tough not having someone on her team, someone she could depend on for emotional support during a trying day. But Diana had learned the hard way that it was much easier to live on her own, relying only on herself.

As she stood at the sink, washing and peeling potatoes, she glanced out the window, where, beyond the brick wall, she could see Zack sitting in the cab of his tractor, hard at work.

Becky was right. He was certainly handsome. And he had one of those don't-mess-with-me auras. Something that suggested he hadn't been pampered.

He reminded her of Travis Dayton, a rebellious teenage boy she'd once known, who smoked, drank and rode a motorcycle with a gutted muffler. There'd been something daring and dangerous about Travis, something wild and forbidden that, as a high school good girl, she'd found attractive. And one night, she'd nearly made the biggest mistake of her life.

At the time, she'd gotten what she considered a divine appeal, one of those once in a lifetime get-out-of-hell-free cards. And there was no way she'd risk throwing caution to the wind again.

The engine of the dozer groaned as it worked in the field. And Diana couldn't help studying the young, brawny operator who was still shirtless. She wondered if he'd been genetically blessed with those muscles or whether hard work had done the job for him.

It had been a long time since a guy with an edge had turned her head. But Diana knew better than to get involved with anyone again. Not even a kind and gentle man like Peter Lynch, the minister she'd married.

In his own way, Peter had been a disappointment, too. But that was her secret. She'd never let the girls know their father hadn't been the perfect man that had been engrained in their memories.

Just the other night, while tucking her daughters into bed and listening to their prayers, Jessie had asked God for a new daddy to make their family complete. But Diana hadn't been able to utter an amen to that.

She didn't want another husband. Every man who'd ever loved her, every man she should have been able to depend upon, had disappointed her or hurt her, in one way or another.

No, a new husband and a stepfather wouldn't make their lives complete.

She might have believed so once upon a time, but she'd put away girlish dreams years ago.

Yet, for some silly reason, she couldn't help looking out the kitchen window one last time.

Chapter Two

The next day, Zack continued to work on his own until two mechanics showed up on the site to set up a ten thousand-gallon drop tank that would provide water for dust control and compaction. He cleared a suitable spot near the water main and the entrance on Callaway Drive, which wasn't far from the brick wall where Becky and Jessie had watched him yesterday.

But the girls hadn't shown their faces today. He figured that after he'd handed over Jessie to her mom and gone back to work, Diana had told her daughters to stay away from the construction site completely. Or maybe the girls had just lost interest in the dirt and dust. He certainly couldn't blame them if they had.

After the mechanics left, he continued to work alone. But he didn't mind. Keeping busy helped the week to pass until he could again spend a couple of hours with his daughter.

Ever since his parole, his life and Sunday afternoons had taken on a whole new meaning.

Some people might not understand why Zack hadn't sought full custody and taken Emily from the foster mother who'd raised her. He'd meant to, while he was still in prison, but when he was released and met his four-year-old daughter for the very first time, he didn't have the heart to upset her little world and take her from a loving home.

Besides, Caitlin Tanner, Emily's foster mom, should be named Bayside Mother of the Year.

Of course, that didn't mean Zack didn't want to spend more time with Emily. Or that he wasn't trying his damnedest to be a good father. But truthfully, he still felt a little awkward around her, since he didn't know jack squat about kids, especially girls.

Little by little he was learning, though—every Sunday afternoon.

He turned the dozer and moved to the far side of the field, away from the bordering neighborhood. Every now and then he glanced toward Becky and Jessie's backyard. They were obviously obedient kids. He would have been, too, if he'd had a mother like theirs.

Just after eleven, he looked toward the water tank.

And this time, he spotted their faces peering over the wall, their hands clutching the gray, roughened cinder blocks.

He probably should ignore them so they'd return to the house and do something other than watch him work, but he decided to head over there and remind them of what their mother had said. He didn't want them to get forgetful and climb to the top of the wall as the day progressed.

As he neared the girls, it was impossible to hear their voices over the drone of the diesel engine, but eager waves and lip movements made it easy to decipher a greeting.

Their childish enthusiasm tickled him, and he waved back. Then he set down the blade, placed the gear into Neutral and climbed from the rig.

"Hi, Zack!" Jessie started to wave, then her eyes widened. "Oops!" She gasped and wobbled from whatever she'd perched on, then quickly grabbed the wall to steady herself.

"You girls need to be careful," he admonished, his voice loud enough to be heard over the noise. "I thought your mother said you weren't supposed to climb up there."

"We *aren't* climbing on the wall," the older girl said. "We're standing on stuff."

Their yard sat higher than the field where Zack stood. But at his height, he had no trouble peering over the six-foot barrier, which was probably only two-thirds as high on their side. They stood on a tri-cycle and a wagon.

"I'm not sure that your mother would approve of this, either," he said. "Where's your baby-sitter?"

"Megan?" Jessie, the younger girl, blew out a big sigh and rolled her eyes. "She used to play with us when Mommy went to work. But now that she got a new cell phone for her birthday, all she ever does is talk to her friends about boys and parties."

Becky tossed a long strand of blond hair over her shoulder. "She's a teenager. You know how it is."

No, Zack didn't figure he knew much about teen-age girls. Or about babysitters. But he didn't think Diana was paying Megan to chat on the phone and leave her daughters to fend for themselves.

He, himself, was just learning how to parent. God knew he'd never had a decent role model, other than his grandmother in the early years. And try as he might, he really couldn't remember as much as he'd like to.

So he tried to imagine the way Emily's foster mom would handle a situation like this. Caitlin was really fussy when it came to Emily's care—something that gave him great peace of mind.

"Want a snack?" Jessie asked. "We made cookies for you last night, after Mommy washed the dishes."

"Your mom made cookies for me?"

"No," Jessie said. "She made them for our lunch this week. But me and Becky saved some for you."

For a moment, a stupid little thrill had shot through him, thinking that the girls' attractive mother had made cookies for him. But he should have known better, especially when talking to kids. Emily had an interesting way of looking at things and came up with some real doozies sometimes.

"They're oatmeal raisin cookies with nuts," the older girl—Becky—added. "They're very healthy and good for you. Our mom is big on things like that."

He figured she would be. "Oatmeal raisin, huh?" He'd lived with his grandmother in Escondido when he was a kid, but not long enough to create more than a few faded memories.

Homemade cookies, fresh out of the oven, had been one of them.

Zack had always had a sweet tooth, although he'd usually appeased it with the candy he hid in the glove box of his Camaro. But a snack made by the girls and their mother sounded pretty darn tempting. "You know, I'd really like a cookie. But it'll have to wait for lunch. I don't want to make my foreman angry if he shows up and I'm loafing on the job."

"What's a foreman?" little Jessie asked.

"My boss."

She nodded her head sagely. "Oh, I get it. Like Reverend Morton."

Was she talking about a minister? Zack didn't get the comparison, unless old Reverend Morton was full of dos and don'ts.

"Is he pretty bossy?" Zack asked.

"Nope. He's pretty nice, as far as pastors go," Becky said, as though she had a wealth of experience with ministers. "He's our mom's boss."

Their mother worked at a church? He supposed a job like that suited her.

"Our mom is the office manager," Jessie said. "And she works on the computer and answers the phone. And she knows everything about what happens at church. Reverend Morton said she's a real blessing. And he can't get along without her."

Zack wondered if Reverend Morton was old or young, married or single. Then he kicked himself for giving a rip about something like that. Why should he care? Diana was the kind of woman who'd attract a preacher. And if she had? Good for her and the girls.

"Reverend Morton likes our mom a whole lot," Becky said.

Oh, yeah? How much was a whole lot?

"He's a very nice man," the older girl added, "but he's not her type."

What *was* her type? Zack wondered.

A convicted felon certainly wasn't, but no need to get into that.

"Well," he said. "I need to get back to work. But I'm going to eat lunch in the shade of the water tank. We can talk then."

"Okay," the girls said in unison.

"And be careful climbing down," he advised them, using what he hoped was a paternal tone.

Thirty minutes later, Zack broke for lunch. He'd no more than kicked back in the shade, bit into the pastrami sandwich he'd fixed himself and taken a swig of the lemonade he'd made out of a powdered mix when the girls returned. Again, they used their toys to help them peer over the wall.

He passed on the milk they offered him, but the chewy cookies were out of this world. "These are great."

"Thank you," Becky said.

"Our mom helped us. And she's the bestest cooker in the whole, wide world," Jessie added. "She's going to make meat loaf tonight, 'cause it's my favorite."

"I don't know about that," the older girl corrected. "Mom's going to get home pretty late. And I bet we have to eat soup and sandwiches like last time."

Was the widowed church secretary going out after work? That seemed a little surprising, although he didn't know much about nice women like her. Maybe she and the Bible thumper had a thing going.

"Why is she coming home late?" he asked, immediately wishing he hadn't.

"She has to take the bus home," Jessie said. "That's how she got to work today. The car is broken again."

He didn't doubt it. That old Plymouth had sounded as though it was on its last wheel when she'd come home yesterday.

"She's probably going to be riding the bus for a long time," the older girl said. "She can't afford to have someone fix the car yet."

"That's all right," the younger girl said. "Riding the bus is really fun."

It might be fun for a child. And public transportation was certainly an option. But Zack doubted their mother was happy about not having a dependable car.

"How far away is your mom's work?" he asked.

"About twenty minutes when she drives us to church," Becky said. "But it takes a lot longer on the bus, because it's all the way in San Diego, and we have to take two or three different ones, just to get there."

For a moment he thought about a darkened bus stop in the bad part of town. A pregnant woman waiting alone, trying to catch the 209 home. A dark sedan driving by. The glint of metal. A gunshot. A body slumping to the ground. A pool of blood. Screams. Sirens.

It had been a fluke. A random shooting that wasn't likely to happen again.

He'd been locked up, unable to help Teresa. Unable to sit with a premature baby. Unable to do anything but stare at the damned bars that had imprisoned him.

Zack blew out a sigh. Maybe he ought to check out that rusted out old clunker Diana drove. He was a pretty decent mechanic and knew a guy down at the auto junkyard where he got used parts at a discount.

He reached into the bag of barbecue chips, but paused before sticking one in his mouth. "After work,

I'll take a look at your mom's car. Maybe I can get it running again."

"That's way cool," Becky said. "My mom is going to think you're a real live hero."

With his record and his past, Zack was about as far from hero material as a man came, especially in the eyes of a pretty widow who worked as a church secretary.

It was almost seven o'clock when Diana finally started down Shady Lane to the small rented home where she and the girls lived.

She wished she'd worn walking shoes rather than heels, but when the car engine wouldn't turn over this morning, she'd been afraid to take the time to run inside for a pair of tennies or flats. If she couldn't make it to the bus stop by eight o'clock, she would have had to wait another thirty minutes for the 213. As it was, she'd power-walked and had to run the last fifty yards.

The sun had lowered over the Pacific, but due to a hurricane off the coast of Mexico, there wasn't the usual ocean breeze to cool the sultry air. After two long bus rides and a five-block walk, her clothes were clinging to her damp skin. She tugged at her silky blouse and shifted the long strap of her purse to the other shoulder.

Jessie had asked for meat loaf and mashed potatoes for dinner, but there was no way Diana would turn on the oven tonight. In fact, she planned to take a shower and slip on a pair of shorts and a tank top as soon as she got home.

As she neared her driveway, she spotted the opened hood of her car and a hulk of a man bent over the engine. Her daughters stood at his side.

Zack?

Her heart fluttered, and she'd be darned if she wanted to contemplate why.

When Jessie glanced down the street, she let out a shriek. "Mommy's home." Then she ran down the sidewalk with open arms, welcoming Diana home with a child-size bear hug.

Diana wrapped her youngest child in a warm embrace. "What's going on, Jes?"

"Zack is the best car fixer in the whole wide world. And he's going to fix ours for free. Isn't he nice?"

"It sure looks that way." She took Jessie's hand and continued home, aware of the way her bra stuck to her skin, the way her blouse clung to her chest and arms. Aware that she needed to comb her hair and apply a light coat of lipstick.

She tried to use the excuse of the weather, physical exertion and being hot and tired as a reason to dash inside and freshen up.

But she was having a hard time buying into that explanation, especially when the tall, dark and ruggedly handsome man pushed away from the car to face her.

He wore a T-shirt this evening, yet she could still

see the flex of his muscles as he slowly lifted his head from the car and turned.

His size alone was enough to make a woman catch her breath. But that's not the only thing that caused sexual awareness to build into a slow and steady rush.

A shank of unruly dark hair taunted her to brush it off his forehead. And a sky-is-the-limit gaze lanced her to the core. A square cut jaw suggested he could take it on the chin—and probably had, more times than not.

His lips quirked in a boyish half smile, and he nodded at the worn-out sedan. "I hope you don't mind that I took a look under the hood."

"No. Not at all." She tucked a strand of hair behind her ear, feeling a bit awkward. Shy. Self-conscious.

How could she have such a silly, adolescent reaction to a stranger who was only being a Good Samaritan?

The screen door squeaked, and Megan walked outside. "How was your day at work, Mrs. Lynch?"

"It was fine." The trek home had been a bit bothersome. But other than that, Diana couldn't complain. At least she had a job. And Reverend Morton had been more than understanding about her plight. In fact, he'd wanted to give her a ride home, but he'd had a meeting with the deacons at five-thirty.

"Well," the teen said, reaching for her backpack that sat just inside the door. "I guess I'd better go."

"Thank you for looking after the girls. Can you please come a half an hour earlier tomorrow? I'll need to take the bus again."

"Sure." The teenager turned toward the Plymouth. "It's too bad about your car."

Diana merely nodded in response. The trusty vehicle had gotten them from Texas to California without any mishaps. And she ought to be thankful it had broken down in the driveway, rather than on the interstate. At least she'd saved money on a towing bill.

"If it makes you feel better," Zack said, "I think I can get it running. But I'll need a few parts."

"I hate to put you out."

"No problem." Those baby blues locked on her again, this time drawing her in like a fisherman reeling in his catch—hook, line and sinker.

The intensity of the tenuous connection made her overly conscious of the moisture gathering under her arms, made her wish she'd run a brush through her hair before leaving the bus stop, maybe sprayed on a light splash of perfume.

For a woman who had absolutely no intention of allowing another man back in her life, how crazy was that?

She cleared her throat, hoping to gain control over her pulse and her wits. "I'm afraid my budget is pretty stretched right now."

"Don't worry about it. And although this car won't make it much longer, I think I can get it running, at least temporarily, without too much effort. If you make me a batch of oatmeal cookies, we'll call it even."

"Mom," Becky said, tugging at the sleeve of Diana's blouse, "shouldn't we invite Zack for dinner, too?"

"That's not necessary," he said, as though sensing Diana's surprise at her daughter's invitation. "I'll get something on my way to the auto parts store."

She ought to let it go, maybe even ask him to dinner tomorrow night instead. But it had been nice of him to look at her car. God knew she couldn't afford a mechanic for another couple of weeks. She was still paying off Becky's dental work.

"We're not having anything special," she told him with a smile. "But I'd be happy if you'd share dinner with us."

He seemed to ponder the offer. Or maybe he was just trying to come up with a way to bow out gracefully. Then he gave her a slow, boyish shrug. "If you're sure it's no problem."

"Not at all," she said, although her heart was thumping to a primitive jungle beat. And that sounded a little problematic to her. "It'll take me a few minutes, though. Do you mind waiting?"

"Nope. I'll just drive down to the auto parts store and see if they've got a new battery."

She froze in her tracks. If her math was correct, her check register boasted all of forty-seven dollars and thirteen cents to last her until next payday. "What will a new battery cost?"

"No more than fifty bucks, I'd say. But I'm going to put it on my credit card. I won't need payment for another three weeks or so."

She whispered a quick prayer, thanking God for looking out for her, even though she'd done her share of grumbling and complaining on the walk to the bus stop this morning. "Do you mind taking a postdated check?"

"Nope. Not at all." He dropped the hood of the car, then swiped his hands together twice. "I'll be back in a few minutes."

As he strode down the street, she called out, "Wait a minute. Where's your car? You're not on foot, too, are you?"

He slid her a heart-strumming grin. "Nope. My car is parked on the job site."

Then he continued on his way.

She didn't know how long she had before he returned, hungry and ready to eat. But she decided a quick jump in the shower would make standing over a hot stove so much more bearable.

The thought that she might want to freshen up for more reasons than the heat and humidity crossed her mind, but she quickly brushed it aside. She wouldn't put her heart on the line again.

The girls had hinted that they'd all be much happier when Diana found another husband. But Diana knew better than that.

Sometimes men placed demands and stress upon a woman in ways the outside world could never imagine.

Zack didn't have a credit card, but he wasn't about to tell Diana that. He would loan her the money for as long as she needed. In fact, if he could figure out a graceful way of making a gift out of it, he would.

So he purchased a heavy-duty battery and took it back to her house, where he put it in the car. He also replaced her spark plugs and put in a new fuel filter. All in all, it cost him more than a hundred dollars, but what the hell.

It made him feel good to help out the little family.

And he'd be getting a home-cooked dinner out of the deal, too. A guy couldn't complain about that.

When he'd made sure the engine was running, he shut off the ignition, closed the car door and lowered the hood. Then he washed up at the faucet in front of the house. Maybe he should have asked for a rain check for a night when he could shower at home and come dressed appropriately.

But then again, he wouldn't be surprised if Diana reneged on tonight's dinner offer. Until very recently, his life had been one big disappointment after another.

That is, until two of the greatest guys he'd ever met had stepped up to the plate.

Bob Adams, his boss, for one. When Zack was a teen, the guy had taken an interest in him when no one else had, letting him borrow tools and work on an old pickup that most people thought would never run again. A beat-up, twenty-two-year-old truck he'd traded in on a '67 Camaro when he'd gotten out of prison.

And when it seemed that no one in Bayside believed his story about being in the wrong place at the wrong time, Bob had believed him. He'd even come out to visit Zack at the Riverview Correctional Facility when no one else had.

The other man was Harry Logan, a detective who'd tried to help a miserable, hard-ass teenager who'd had more than his share of trouble with the law. Some of the things Harry had told Zack had finally taken root, but Harry hadn't known that. Not when Zack had headed out to meet the cop one evening and ended up behind bars and on the six o'clock news.

When Zack was paroled, Harry had reached out again, welcoming Zack into a brotherhood of men known as Logan's Heroes, a group of misfit delinquents who'd turned their sorry lives around because of Harry's guidance and influence.

With guys like Bob and Harry on his side, Zack's future was looking up.

The present, however, was another story.

As Zack stood before Diana's door, he took a deep breath, then slowly blew it out. For some reason, a swarm of butterflies had swooped through his gut, and he wasn't sure why. It's not like this was a date or anything. He pulled open the screen, then knocked lightly.

Jessie and Becky struggled to be the first to let him inside a small but homey living room with mismatched furniture, where framed photographs lined the mantel over the fireplace.

"I'll go tell my mom you're here," the older girl said, before dashing off.

All of a sudden, in spite of a whiff of something that smelled tasty and tempted a grumble from his belly, Zack had second thoughts about accepting this dinner invitation. He'd eaten with the Logans a few times and with Brett and Caitlin Tanner once or twice, but he still felt kind of weird in those sit-down-at-the-table situations.

When the pretty brunette entered the living room, wearing a pair of white shorts, a red sleeveless blouse and a heart-spinning smile, he couldn't have conjured a reason to leave, even if he'd tried.

There was an old adage that said beauty was only skin deep. But Zack had a feeling Diana's went clear to the bone.

"Hi," she said.

Rather than slip into chitchat, which would make him uneasy, he grappled to find a safe conversation, something that promoted his self-confidence. "The car is running again. I'm not sure how long it will last before you'll need to buy something newer, but it ought to get you to work and back for the time being."

"Thank you." She placed her hands on her hips, drawing his attention to her gentle curves and making him feel as though he'd crossed some divine line between right and wrong, Heaven and hell.

He tried to shrug off his inappropriate interest. "I like tinkering with engines and have a knack for mechanics. Always have. In fact, I bought an old, beat-up Camaro and have been fixing it up. I rebuilt the engine, and now it runs like a charm. It doesn't look too pretty on the outside, but it will—someday."

Crap. He hadn't meant to spout off like that. He hoped she didn't think he was boasting. But it wasn't easy talking to a lady like her.

Hell, he'd never been tongue-tied around women before. Of course, his dates had always been a bit rough and ragged around the edges and not at all like Diana. And even if he was getting his life on track, getting his focus out of the gutter and on the kind of future that would make his daughter proud of him someday, he couldn't see chasing after a woman like her.

"I don't know how to thank you," she said. "My dad gave me that old car when we lived with him in Texas, and it was pretty worn-out then. But he managed to keep it running for me."

"Is he a mechanic?"

"By necessity. He's actually a trucker."

Zack nodded, as though it made perfect sense. But it merely made him realize how very little he knew about the widowed mother of two. "What brought you out to California?"

Before she could answer, Jessie spoke up. "Mommy worked at a ranch. She counted all their money. But we had to move."

Had she lost her job? Been falsely accused of something, like he'd been? God knew he didn't like people digging into his past. Of course, that didn't make him any less curious about hers.

"Becky," the soft-spoken mother said to the older girl, "why don't you and your sister set the table out on the patio. It's a bit warm to eat inside."

"Cool. Jessie and I like it when we eat outdoors. Can I light the bug candle, too?"

"Not until I'm there to supervise."

The girls dashed off, and Diana took a seat on a worn plaid recliner. She sat at the edge of the cushion, leaning forward slightly, hands on her knees.

She looked ready to bolt.

Silence stretched between them until she said, "You start work pretty early each day."

Okay, so she'd turned the conversation away from her reasons for moving to California. He took the hint and let it drop. "I start at seven o'clock. In the next few days, the rest of the crew will join me. And I'm afraid the equipment will only get louder."

"That's all right. My alarm goes off about that time. And the noise from your bulldozer just reminds me to get in the shower."

Zack doubted he'd ever fire up that engine again without glancing in the direction of Diana's house and wondering if she was awake.

And headed for the shower.

He envisioned the shapely brunette taking off a white cotton gown and stepping under the gentle spray of a warm shower. Naked. Water sluicing over her.

"So," he said, trying to squelch the sexual curiosity that seemed sinful in the case of a widowed church secretary and the mother of two. "Do you like living in Bayside better than Texas?"

"Yes, but we really miss our friends, the Merediths. They were like family to us."

"What made you move?" Okay, so he was prodding her, when turnabout wasn't fair play.

"We were living with my father and..." She glanced in the direction the girls had run. "He's a good man, but critical to a fault. And I had to put a little distance between him and the girls. I didn't want them to grow up in a harsh environment."

The kind of environment she'd grown up in, no doubt. But she seemed to have come away unscathed.

"Well," she said, nodding toward the kitchen. "If you'll excuse me for a minute, I have to check something on the stove."

"Sure." He watched her walk away, unable to ignore the gentle sway of her rounded hips. He blew out a pent-up sigh, hoping to shake off the attraction that brewed under his surface.

He glanced at the lamp table, spotting a framed photograph of a smiling man and woman.

A groom and his pretty, brown-haired bride.

Diana and her husband.

The girls had said their father passed away. They seemed to be okay with the loss. But how about their mother?

Was she still grieving? Still brokenhearted?

He hoped not. Diana was too young, too sweet, too perfect to be hurting.

And too damned young to be sleeping alone.

Again, he cursed his sexual attraction to a woman who was way out of his reach.

Chapter Three

Diana stood at the stove. As spaghetti sauce simmered over a low flame, she stared at a large pot of water, wondering if it would ever boil.

On the way home from the bus stop, she'd thought about fixing canned soup and sandwiches for dinner—something quick and easy. But she couldn't very well serve a light meal like that to a construction worker the size of Paul Bunyon and with, she imagined, an appetite to match.

So she'd used the hamburger she'd set aside for meat loaf and added a jar of store-bought marinara she kept on hand for emergencies like this.

But she couldn't very well let Zack wait alone in

the living room, without even the girls to entertain him. So she left the pots, one simmering and the other on high, and headed back to her guest.

He sat on the worn, tweed sofa, studying a photograph of her and Peter on their wedding day.

When he heard her enter the room, he returned the silver frame to the lamp table, tossed her a half smile and nodded at the twelve-year-old picture that spoke of another time, another life. "I hope you don't mind."

"No, of course not." She'd left that picture out for her daughters' benefit, along with a couple of others down the hall.

"The girls told me your husband…their dad… passed away."

She nodded. "About two years ago."

"I'm sorry."

Most people felt awkward discussing death and loss, and for some reason, Diana wanted to make it easy on Zack. And easy on herself. "Time heals. And we've adjusted pretty well. At least, I think the girls are doing all right."

Compassion spread across his face, and she realized he assumed she hadn't gotten over *her* loss. But that's not what she'd meant.

She took a seat in the easy chair that had, along with the other furniture, come with the house. "I'm doing all right, too."

And she was. Her husband had been one of the

kindest, gentlest men she'd ever known, but she'd gotten over his death easier than her daughters had.

She'd loved him, of course. How could she not? But she'd never really felt his love in return. His focus had always been on the church rather than on her and the girls. And, after a while, she'd grown to resent the time he spent trying to nurture everyone else in the small, struggling congregation.

So after holding down the home front by herself for what had seemed like forever, she continued to do the same after his death. And if truth be told—

Oh, God. It sounded so terrible to admit, but there hadn't been a lot for her to miss.

At times, she wondered if she'd bypassed a step in the grieving process. But in reality, she'd probably been so busy trying to keep the wolf from the door that she'd passed through it all without a backward glance.

"What was his name?" Zack asked.

"Peter."

"How did he die?"

"From a heart attack. And since he was only thirty-four, he probably overlooked any symptoms he might have had." She fingered the frayed, braided edge on the armrest of the chair. "Late one evening, the church janitor found him slumped over his desk."

"Wow." The word came out as a solemn whisper.

She didn't want Zack feeling sorry for them. It happened; they'd survived. End of story.

"Peter was a good man," she told him. "And he's in a better place."

"Better than being with a beautiful wife and two great kids?" He frowned. Then he softened. "Sorry. Just my cynical nature busting loose."

Over the past few years, Diana had grown a little cynical, too, although she usually hid it well. She offered Zack a smile that was steeped more in hope than reality. "Please don't be sorry. Life goes on."

He nodded, yet that awkwardness she'd wanted to avoid settled over them. She assumed it was due in part to them being strangers. Or, then again, maybe she was feeling uneasy about the thoughts she was usually so good at suppressing.

Yet there seemed to be something else happening, too. Something that had a lot to do with them being male and female.

It had been a long time since a man had held her in his arms. Maybe that's why she found this virtual stranger so darn attractive, even though she had no intention of replacing the man she'd lost.

Death, they said, had a way of memorializing a person, making them seem almost saintly, when in reality, they'd been flawed and human. But in Peter's case, that hadn't happened. Not for her, anyway. He'd lost his footing on the pedestal on which she'd placed him years ago.

"The girls say you're a secretary," Zack said, obviously wanting to change the subject as badly as she did.

"Yes, I am. A friend from college knew I was looking to relocate, and she told me there was a perfect position for me at the Park Avenue Community Church. I interviewed over the phone, and Reverend Morton went to bat for me with the board of elders. Two days later, he offered me the job. And here we are."

"I hear he can't get along without you." Zack didn't know why he mentioned what the girls had told him, why he felt compelled to turn the conversation toward the preacher. But the fact was, he wanted to hear that the good reverend was seventy years old and happily married.

"Tom, or rather Pastor Morton, is a very busy man. And he appreciates someone taking care of the little things for him. I'm sure another secretary would be just as helpful."

Before Zack could think of a response, the two girls entered the living room. It didn't take long to figure out they'd been eavesdropping.

"Mrs. Ashton says our mom is perfect for the job because she used to be a pastor's wife and knows just what to do to make Reverend Morton's life easier," Becky interjected.

Diana's husband used to be a preacher?

Somehow, that didn't surprise him. And, if anything, it only placed Diana on a higher level than most people.

When he was younger, before his time in prison, he'd never dated anyone who was considered a good girl, even though he'd sensed one or two of them had been attracted to him. It didn't take a psychic to see the conflict in a mismatched relationship like that.

And from what he'd already seen and easily surmised, women didn't get much nicer than Diana.

"Mrs. Ashton said Reverend Morton wants to ask Mom out on a date," Becky said.

"Without us," Jessie interjected. "But Mommy told Mrs. Ashton that she wasn't interested."

"That's because she could do *way* better than him."

"Girls, that's enough. Mrs. Ashton is well-intentioned, but she has entirely too big of an imagination." Diana glanced at Zack, her embarrassment reflected by rosy cheeks. "There are a few people in this world who live by a Noah's Ark philosophy."

A smile tugged at Zack's lips. "What's that?"

"The idea that this world would be a much better place if everyone made the journey two-by-two. But I don't agree."

He wondered why. Had she been so in love with her husband that she couldn't imagine another man taking his place?

If so, it made sense.

Diana looked at Zack. "Do you mind supervising while Becky lights the candle on the patio table?"

"No. Not at all." He got to his feet and allowed the girls to lead him through a small dining room and out a sliding door to a patio, where they'd set the table for four. The truth was, he was glad to have something to do. Glad to have something to focus on.

Something other than a woman who needed what she'd once had—the kind of man Zack would never be.

For some dumb reason, in spite of two little kids sitting at the table, the evening held a romantic aura Zack found hard to ignore.

Maybe it was because of the faint scent of night-blooming jasmine, the air rustling the leaves in the tree, a full moon overhead.

Of course, the attractive woman sitting at his side held an aura of her own.

The flicker of two candles lit the small patio table, as forks clicked against ceramic dinnerware.

Zack dug into a plate filled high with spaghetti, hoping he didn't dribble sauce all down his chin and on his shirt. He'd never been self-conscious while eating before. But this meal was different, and he hoped what few manners he'd acquired during his youth hadn't been lost after five long years behind bars.

"Thanks for including me," he told Diana. "The girls were right. You're a good cook."

"You should eat her meat loaf and mashed potatoes," Jessie said. "I always eat a hundred helpings."

"You'll have to come over for dinner when Mom makes chicken-fried steak," Becky added. "It's really good, too."

Zack glanced at Diana, saw her flush again. Was she embarrassed by the praise?

Or by the possibility that the girls would offer Zack another dinner invitation he might accept?

"I haven't had many home-cooked meals," he admitted. "But this is one of the best."

"Thank you."

As their gazes caught, her movements stilled.

His, too.

Something hovered in the night air. Sexual awareness, he suspected—something she'd sensed, too. But she looked away, cleared her throat and scooted her chair from the table. "Ice cream anyone? It's Rocky Road."

The girls eagerly placed their orders. And since Zack was big on dessert and chocolate was his favorite, he shot her a grin. "Sure. I'd like some. Thanks."

When Diana went inside, Becky rested her elbows on the table, leaned forward and whispered, "Even if Mom wanted to go on a date, it wouldn't be with Reverend Morton. He's not her type. And not just because he's going to be totally bald someday."

Where had that come from? The preacher's name hadn't popped into the conversation since Diana had put a stop to it earlier. Obviously, the child had been holding back her opinion until her mother slipped way.

"When he wears his Padres baseball cap he looks kind of handsome," the younger girl said. "But he doesn't have muscles. Not like yours."

Zack was pleased that the preacher couldn't hold a candle to him—physically, at least. But he figured a woman like Diana was more interested in character and reputation. In that case, Morton had him beat by light years. Not that he was in the running.

Or was he?

Was he being set up by a couple of pint-sized matchmakers?

"You know the Noah's Ark story?" Becky asked.

Not really, but he had a general idea, so he nodded sagely, as if he was an expert.

"The story's true, even if Mom doesn't believe it."

Zack didn't think Diana was questioning the story. She'd just been making a statement about people not needing to be paired off to be happy.

"God is very big on love and marriage," Becky explained. "That's why he made Adam and Eve."

"And it's why He made Noah and…" Jessie paused, screwed up her little face and looked at her all-knowing big sister. "What was his wife's name, Becky?"

"I don't remember. But she was *very* important to the whole story."

As the screen door slid open, the subject immediately dropped—*thank goodness.*

Zack wasn't sure where the blond, starry-eyed preteen was going with all that stuff. But his suspicion about being set up was growing stronger by the minute.

"All right," Diana said, as she carried in a tray with four bowls. "Here it is."

He found safety in the silence that followed, as Becky and Jessie grabbed their spoons and dug into the frozen concoction of chocolate ice cream, marshmallows and nuts.

For some reason, he got the feeling that the girls thought he might make a better catch for their mom than the preacher. But that was only because they didn't have any idea who he was or where he'd been.

It was almost laughable.

Still, Zack couldn't help being glad the preacher wasn't their mother's type.

Nor could he help wondering who was.

His gaze drifted to Diana, whose red T-shirt revealed the kind of breasts many women paid to have. Hers, he suspected, were real. In fact, everything about her was so womanly, so genuine, that it was hard to keep his eyes off her. And, in spite of himself, he stole another peek.

She had her eyes closed, a spoon in her mouth, savoring the sweet, creamy taste and wearing an almost-orgasmic expression that nearly knocked the breath right out of him.

Damn. He'd always thought women got old and frumpy after having kids. But not her.

In the conservative clothes she'd worn to work, she appeared to be fit and trim. But wearing a pair of white shorts and a T-shirt, there wasn't much guesswork involved. She had the best pair of legs he'd ever snuck a peek at.

He figured she was at least thirty and a good five years older than him.

With sea-green eyes and honey-brown hair a man would love to see splayed on his pillow, she was a beautiful woman.

When she opened her eyes and saw him looking at her, the rebel in him tossed her a crooked grin.

She returned his smile, but not before flushing a pretty shade of pink.

Something told him he wasn't the only one who suspected a romantic setup.

Diana had never been so uneasy in her life. Or so embarrassed by her children. Of course, she could understand why the girls were impressed with the handsome construction worker. He was a giant of a man, with a bulky build that suggested he protected what was his. Yet his baby blue eyes boasted a boyish innocence.

And when he'd shot her an I-walk-on-the-wildside grin, it was enough to steal her breath away, not to mention her good sense.

Her daughters wouldn't understand her reluctance to get involved with a man, especially one with a devilish smile that could tempt a woman to pick a forbidden apple and take a bite. But they'd obviously decided their mother needed another man in her life, when that couldn't be further from the truth.

"It's my turn to do the dishes," Becky said, as she

pushed her chair from the table and picked up her empty bowl and spoon. "And Jessie wants to help me."

"But I don't want—"

Becky cleared her throat. *"Yes you do."*

"Oh, yeah," the younger girl said. "I do."

"Come on." Becky led her sister through the sliding door and into the kitchen.

A moment later, Jessie ran back to close the door.

The girls were usually pretty good about helping out in the house—when prodded. But they never took the initiative on their own. There was only one conclusion to make.

Her daughters wanted her to be alone with a man they'd dressed in imaginary armor and placed on a white steed.

But was there any such thing as a real-life hero?

Diana had her doubts. Women often imagined a man was something he wasn't, especially if she was attracted to him. But the truth struck a hard blow.

There was so much more to a man than met the eye.

Of course, in Zack's case, what met the eye was very nice, even with—or maybe because of—a five o'clock shadow that lent him a raw, dangerous air, especially under the spell of candlelight.

Physically, he was the complete opposite of Peter, a man she'd practically handpicked when they were in college because he was so different from the dark-haired hellion who'd nearly ruined her life. She'd also chosen him because he'd been a man she thought her blue-collared, demanding-yet-impossible-to-please father would approve of. So she'd set her sights on the gentle man who hadn't pointed out her every flaw and shortcoming.

Other than one.

She cleared her throat. "I'm afraid my daughters are a little…"

"Eager to find their mother a boyfriend?" he supplied, with a chuckle and a sparkle in his eye.

Thank goodness he'd not only broached the subject, but made light of the obvious, making her daughter's matchmaking so much easier to address—and to set aside.

"I'm afraid Becky has a romantic streak and has spent way too much time reading fairy tales," she explained. "And Jessie just misses having a man around the house, even if it was only for a few minutes a day."

"Their father didn't spend much time with them?"

As had become her habit, she quickly jumped to Peter's defense. "He was trying to build a church and was very busy."

"I guess that's a good excuse," Zack replied. "My dad didn't have any time for me, but his reasons weren't anywhere near as noble."

Diana smiled at their commonality. "My father was a long-haul trucker, so his time at home was pretty limited, too."

There'd been a difference, though. Her father's absence had served to support his family the best way he knew how. To provide for them.

Which was why, to this day, her father resented Peter for leaving her and the girls as poor as the proverbial church mice. And, to be honest, there were times when Diana resented Peter, too.

Anger was part of the grieving process, and she'd been angry with God at first for taking Peter when he'd had such a good heart and had his whole life before him.

But as time passed, that initial anger transferred to her deceased husband, a man who, according to her father, had been so spiritually minded, that he hadn't been any earthly good.

It was only at night, when she lay in bed alone, that she could admit her resentment. And then the guilt set in. How could she find fault with a man like Peter?

Zack leaned forward and lowered his voice to an intimate caress. "Can I ask you a question?"

She glanced across the table, saw the seriousness of his expression and was almost afraid to tell him it was okay to ask. "Sure, go ahead."

"What do you wish your husband would have done with your daughters?" He glanced at his hands, big hands that bore a couple of intriguing scars. Then he returned his gaze to her. "I mean, what kind of things would you have wanted your father to have done with you when you were a child?"

He'd tossed out the question like the kind of verbal bait a counselor used to get to the heart of a person's past, a person's problems.

Or maybe Zack figured they'd both had a less-than-perfect childhood in common.

"It wouldn't have had to be anything big or expensive, like taking a kid to a theme park. A trip to the library would have been nice, followed by a story or two. It wouldn't have hurt him to spend a day at the playground with a picnic lunch. Or to take a walk on the shore and collect pretty rocks." She gave a wistful little shrug of her shoulder. "It's a matter of spending special time with a child. Attending a school play, sitting in the front row, taking pictures and clapping proudly, even if a kid forgot all her lines. Do you know what I mean?"

Zack nodded, even though he wasn't sure he did. He was constantly trying to think of things to do with Emily, the kind of things a daughter would enjoy with her father. But it wasn't easy.

As a kid, he'd moved around too much, from his grandmother's home to a three-year stint with his old man, to foster care, to an uncle who drank himself to sleep each night. So Zack had come up short in knowing what a good father was like.

Hell, during the time he'd lived with his old man, he would have been happy just to know his dad wouldn't throw him against a wall or knock him on his ass for no reason at all.

"I guess I know the kind of things boys like—

video games, playing catch in the park. But men have a harder time relating to girls. Don't you think?"

"Maybe so. But loving a child enough to listen to her, to get an idea of what she might like or dislike, would be the first step."

He was already trying to do that. Emily liked going to the zoo. And playing on that big, colorful climbing structure at Burger Bob's. But he was hoping to take her someplace Caitlin and Brett hadn't already gone. Hoping he could come up with something that would be a first for her and him, something that would create a memory that was theirs alone.

He supposed it was a little goofy to feel that way, but Emily was the only thing in his past that he was actually proud of, even though his contribution, so far anyway, had only been genetic.

But he wasn't ready to admit to Diana that he had a daughter. A kid someone else was raising because Zack had gone to prison when he was nineteen.

Besides, Diana was probably one of the most perfect women he'd ever met. And just knowing she had an ex-con in her house might upset her.

So, as much as he'd like to be honest with her and as happy as he was to have a sweet little girl like Emily, he kept his mouth shut.

"So tell me about you," she said. "I know you drive a bulldozer. Do you enjoy your work?"

"Yeah. A lot. I like being outdoors." He especially

liked fresh air and sunshine. Prison had left him feeling a bit claustrophobic when indoors.

She leaned forward. "What kind of things do you do in your spare time?"

"I tinker on my car. And I read a lot." Reading had been a habit he'd picked up while in Riverview. Back then it had helped him pass the time. He supposed it still did. He couldn't wait until his parole was up and his life was his own again.

And that was another reason he had no business being here, pretending to be something he wasn't.

"Well," he said, pushing his chair from the table and getting to his feet. "I'd better get home and turn in. My alarm goes off pretty early in the morning. Thanks for inviting me to dinner."

"You're welcome. Thanks for getting my car running. If you'll wait a minute, I'll get you that check for the battery."

He nodded, although he figured he'd just tear it up when he got out to his car. He didn't want her to repay him— not when he suspected her paycheck never stretched far enough.

She followed him into the house, single file, rather than two-by-two, which reminded him of the Noah's Ark stuff that had been discussed earlier. The idea that people needed to go through life in pairs.

Zack suspected that, if there was some kind of divine plan, it had to do with parents and children. With family units.

After telling the girls goodbye and waiting for Diana to add her signature on a check he wouldn't cash, he made his way to the front door.

Her scent, something soft and alluring, taunted him.

"Good night," she said.

It had been, he supposed. "Maybe I'll see you around sometime."

She nodded, and he left.

But as he strode down the sidewalk and to the Camaro he'd parked at the curb, he suddenly felt more alone than he'd ever been.

And Zack had been alone for as long as he could remember.

Chapter Four

Zack had worked by himself for the last time on Saturday, but he hadn't minded. When the rest of the crew began to trickle in next week, he'd be able to enjoy the various personalities that made up Bayside Construction—at least, during lunch and after work.

Neither Becky nor Jessie had shown up at all that day. He suspected that was because Diana had weekends off. Maybe she'd kept them inside. Or maybe she'd taken them somewhere.

It really didn't matter. He had a job to do and didn't need the distraction, no matter how entertaining the girls had been.

At quitting time, he'd gone to the gym, then picked up tacos at a drive-through. He didn't go out much, like he had in his troublemaking days. He was too tried after work and too determined to keep his nose clean. After all, look what had happened to him the last time he'd been at the wrong place at the wrong time.

So he went through the motions until Sunday morning rolled around.

At about twenty minutes before noon, Zack parked his Camaro in a guest parking space at the Ocean Breeze condominium complex, climbed from the car and strode toward the white stucco buildings that sat amidst parklike lawns and tropical plants. He followed the hibiscus-lined sidewalk to the Tanners' front door.

As he stood before the woven, heart-shaped welcome mat, he lifted his hand and knocked lightly.

He was a little early, but he hoped that wouldn't be a problem. It had been a week since he'd seen his daughter.

Of course, he called her every evening and talked to her before bedtime. The nightly calls had been Caitlin's idea, and they'd quickly become something both Zack and Emily looked forward to.

Emily opened the door, wearing a white blouse, pink pants and a bright-eyed grin. "Hi, Daddy."

"Hey, Sunshine."

She raised her arms, and he lifted her up.

When she was at eye level, she said, "I've been waiting for you to come ever since I woke up."

He'd been waiting, too—ever since last Sunday afternoon when he'd dropped her off. "I've been watching the clock, too. But we don't have to wait any longer."

Zack still found it hard to believe he'd had anything to do with this beautiful child's creation. Other than big blue eyes the same color as his, she favored her biological mother. And oddly enough, she also bore an uncanny resemblance to Caitlin, the woman who'd loved and raised her.

"Come in and talk to Mommy so we can go," she told him. Then she called her mother. "Daddy Zack is here."

"I'll be right there," Caitlin answered from the other room.

He carried Emily into the neat and clean living room that smelled of the potpourri Caitlin displayed in crystal bowls.

The Tanners had gotten new furniture since he'd been here last week. The sofa was a solid green, with a floral design woven into the fabric. It was nice. Caitlin sure had an eye for decor and knew how to make a house a home.

Would Diana decorate in the same manner, if her budget wasn't so tight? Probably. He'd sensed something similar in the two women. Some maternal quality that helped them make a place feel comfortable and homey, whether it had new furniture or not.

"Daddy, do you know what?" Emily asked.

He tossed her a grin, eager to be invited into her little-girl world. "No. What?"

"Mommy took me to visit my new school, and I got to meet my teacher, Miss Kathy. Then I got to see the playground. And you know what? You would really *love* it. There's a great big slide and a swing and a sandbox." Her eyes widened and a grin tugged at her little lips. "And guess what else."

He didn't have a clue, but he wanted in on her excitement. "I can't even imagine. Tell me."

"There's a little playhouse with a kitchen inside, where we can cook pretend food, like pizza and bacon and hamburgers."

"That's great. I'll bet you'll have fun playing and meeting a lot of new friends."

Emily nodded, eyes bright.

Caitlin had mentioned putting her in preschool a couple of mornings a week. Apparently, she'd found one that she approved of. He didn't know squat about that kind of stuff, but he trusted that Caitlin had done a lot of research before the visit.

"Uh-oh," Emily said. "I almost forgot my purse. And it has two quarters and some pennies in it. Can you please put me down so I can go get it?"

"You bet." He placed her on the floor, and she scurried off, just as her mother entered the living room.

"Hi, Zack."

"I'm a little early," he admitted, hoping she'd understand—and figuring she would.

"That's okay. Emily's been ready to go since breakfast."

At one time, Caitlin had wanted to adopt Emily, something Zack had refused to allow. While he'd been in prison, he'd been dead-set on getting his life in order. And since he had a lot of time on his hands, he took college-level courses and managed to earn a bachelor's degree he'd yet to use.

But the first step in his plan, once he got out, had been to get custody of the child he'd never seen.

He'd been prepared for a fight, if necessary. But that was before Brett Tanner had come to visit him at Riverview Correctional Facility.

Brett, who'd later married Caitlin, had pointed out that separating Emily from the only mother she'd ever known would be unfair, if not downright cruel.

And Zack had agreed. He'd had firsthand experience with being uprooted from a loving home.

When Zack was only a couple years older than Emily, social services had removed him from his maternal grandmother's care. Following a court-ordered rehab, his father had cleaned up and gotten married. So someone in the system had decided Zack would be better in a two-parent home, especially since his grandmother had been recently diagnosed with rheumatoid arthritis.

It had been more than just a rough blow when Zack had been removed from Nellie Henderson's care. It had been heartbreaking for both him and the only woman who'd ever really loved him.

And he damn well wasn't about to put his daughter through something like that.

So the grown-ups who loved Emily had managed a compromise. And for the time being, visits on Sunday afternoon were okay with Zack.

Emily, who'd returned to the living room with the strap of a little white purse slung over her shoulder, tapped his thigh. "Where are we going this time, Daddy?"

"I heard about this neat place in Lakeside that has pony rides and a farm animal petting zoo. What do you think?"

"Pony rides?" Her eyes grew wide, then she jumped up and down and clapped her hands. "Yea! I love ponies!"

Emily loved all animals, which is why he'd decided Pistol Pete's would be perfect.

"Do you have a camera?" Caitlin asked him. "I'd really like to have some pictures for her scrapbook."

"I'll get one of those disposable ones after we stop at Burger Bob's for lunch."

Three hours, seven pony rides and forty-two snapshots later, Zack finally managed to talk Emily into leaving Pistol Pete's, a small Wild West-style theme park. But not until she'd made friends with a goat, three rabbits, a pony named Hot Shot, Maxwell the llama and a parrot who was supposed to talk, but only squawked.

"Can we come back another day?" she asked.

"Of course."

He secured Emily in the car seat in back, then climbed behind the wheel.

"Are we going to stop and see Grandma Nellie again?" she asked.

"Yep. Maybe we should take her a chocolate milkshake."

"That's a good idea," Emily said. "She really likes chocolate."

His grandmother had written to him in prison, telling him she was praying for him. Zack hadn't put much stock in that. But it helped to know that someone loved him and believed in him.

When he was paroled, he'd gone to see her in the nursing home where she'd been living for the past ten years. And ever since then, he and Emily ended their Sunday afternoons with a visit to her.

Grandma Nellie didn't get too many visitors, so he tried to stop by as often as he could. He'd been a little worried about taking Emily there on that first day, since he wasn't sure how she'd handle being at a convalescent home. The place had been a little unsettling for Zack until he'd gotten used to it.

But Emily had been a real trouper. In fact, she'd become a kind of mascot for the elderly residents, many of whom were confined to a wheelchair or a walker.

"Grandma Nellie will be happy to see us," Emily said.

"She'll be especially happy to see you, Sunshine."

Ten minutes later, they pulled into the parking lot of the Mountain Meadow Manor. Zack helped Emily from her car seat. Then before reaching for her hand, he picked up the cardboard carrier that held three chocolate shakes.

They entered the assisted living facility and headed for the front desk.

"We've come to see Nellie Henderson," Zack said.

The blond, fifty-something receptionist smiled. "Nellie was hoping you'd come again today. She's out in the rose garden, enjoying the blooms. Apparently, she used to be a member of the rose society when she was younger."

And before arthritis had crippled her.

"Yes, she did. And she loves roses. Thanks." Zack led Emily down the hall and through the doorway that led to the patio.

His grandmother had parked under the shade of a maple tree, her back to the door as she studied a rose bush in full bloom. A harvest-colored afghan was draped over her lap.

She didn't see them at first. And when Emily walked up to greet her, the gray-haired woman broke into a happy smile. "Well, hello there, precious."

"Hi, Grandma Nellie. Me and Daddy went to Pistol Pete's, and I got to ride the ponies. And I got to pet a goat and a little lamb and lots of bunnies."

"That's wonderful," Zack's grandmother said. "When I was a little girl like you, I had a pony of my very own. His name was Pretty Boy."

Emily's eyes brightened. "I'd like a pony of my own." She turned to Zack and laid that smile on him, the one that turned his willpower to mush and made it tough to say no.

"Grandma used to live on a farm," he explained. "So she had plenty of room in the yard for a pony. You live in a condominium, and I live in an apartment."

"But you said one day we were going to have a house with a yard. Remember, Daddy?"

Yes, he remembered. But he had to get a sizable down payment first. "That's quite a way off. But I'll keep the pony in mind, all right?"

"Okay."

Grandma bent forward, her gnarled hand reaching out to gently touch Emily's shoulder. "Mrs. Jessup, the lady you met last time, asked if you would draw a picture for her so she can put it on the wall in her room. She used to be a schoolteacher, and since she doesn't have any children of her own, she misses not seeing artwork."

"I'm a very good colorer," Emily said. "I'll make a whole bunch of pictures for you and your friends."

"We'd love that, sweetheart." Grandma reached

for a strand of Emily's white-blond hair, which was beginning to fall free of her Hello Kitty barrettes. "What pretty hair clips. Mrs. Andrews, the woman who lives down the hall from me, makes colorful bows for her granddaughters. And I've asked her to make some for you, too."

"Me and Mommy like bows and ribbons. I'd better make a picture for Mrs. Andrews, too." Emily blessed her great-grandmother with another smile.

"That would make her very happy."

Zack pulled out one chocolate shake, poked in a straw and handed it to his grandma.

"What a nice surprise, Zack. I love chocolate."

His grandmother used to make fudge at Christmas for people around town—the mailman, the woman at the beauty shop who did her hair, among others.

Zack would give anything to see her in the kitchen again, humming to herself and offering him a taste of homemade treats.

"We like chocolate, too," he told her. "Don't we, Em?"

His little girl nodded as he placed a straw in her shake and handed it to her. He'd probably have to finish hers, but that was okay.

"How's the new job working out?" his grandma asked.

"It's coming along all right. I've been on my own this past week, and Bob seems pleased with my progress. It'll be nice when they start moving in the other equipment on Monday."

"It must have been lonely working alone." His grandmother smiled. "Even for a loner like you."

"It's not too bad. There are a couple of little girls that have befriended me."

"What does befriended mean?" Emily asked.

"They saw me working near their yard and decided to wave and make friends with me."

Emily smiled and a drop of chocolate dribbled down her chin. "What are their names?"

"Becky and Jessie. They're nice girls." They had a nice mom, too. But he didn't see any point in mentioning that.

"Can I play with them someday?" Emily asked. "Please?"

Her question took him aback. The girls would probably get along great, but since he had what he considered an inappropriate attraction to Becky and Jessie's mother, he'd decided to avoid contact with them—if possible.

"Maybe someday," he told her, although he hoped she didn't hold him to it. "I don't see them very often."

And he didn't see Emily very often, either.

They continued to chat with Grandma Nellie for a while, then after wheeling her back inside and promising to see her again next Sunday, Zack and Emily said goodbye and headed for the car.

It had been a great day, but it had ended all too soon. It was time to take his daughter home.

Then it would be seven days before he would see her again. That was a long time, he realized.

Even for a loner like him.

"Hey, Henderson."

Zack, who sat with the crew in the shade of the water tower eating lunch, turned to Eddie Avila, a scraper hand who'd been a member of Local 12 for years and had just hired on with the company.

Eddie nodded toward the wall, where Becky and Jessie peered over the top. The youngest girl wiggled her fingers in a wave directed at Zack.

"Fan club?" Eddie asked.

"Yeah. I guess so." He waved back at the girls, as he continued to munch on one of the bologna sandwiches he'd made.

"Zack?" the older girl called. "Can we ask you something?"

"Sure." He stood and carried his uneaten sandwich with him to the wall. "What's up?"

"Do you know anything about washing machines?" she asked.

Just that they needed a whole lot of quarters to work. "Not really. Why?"

"'Cause water leaked out of ours and the whole house is flooded," little Jessie said.

"Not the *whole* house," her older sister explained.

"But now Mom will have to wash our clothes at the Laundromat until she can have somebody come out and fix it."

"What about calling the landlord?" Zack asked.

"We can't do that," the older girl said. "We don't have to pay very much in rent, but we have to fix everything ourselves. That's the deal."

"Yeah," Jessie added. "That's the deal."

"Mrs. Tomasino, who owns our house, is very old," Becky explained. "And she goes to our church. Because our mom works there and Mrs. Ashton is the one who keeps track of the money and writes all the checks, Mrs. Tomasino lets us and Mrs. Ashton live in her two houses. I think she does it instead of putting money in the offering plate. It's part of the deal."

Zack still wasn't exactly sure what they were talking about. But apparently, the washer was on the blink and Diana was responsible for fixing it. "Maybe, after work, I can come by and look at it for you."

"That would be way cool," Becky said.

"Hey, you guys!" a young, female voice called from the backdoor. "Get down and come in the house now."

"Uh-oh," Jessie said. "That's Megan. We better go, or we'll get in trouble."

Zack was glad the sitter seemed to be keeping a better eye on them this week. He supposed she wasn't sick anymore.

"Be careful," Zack told them.

"We'll see you later," Becky said, as she jumped down and followed her sister to the house.

He popped the rest of his sandwich into his mouth, then headed back to the guys sitting in the shade.

"Do any of you know anything about washing machines that leak?" he asked.

"Could be the pump," Dan Holbrook said.

"My brother-in-law has an appliance repair shop on Hampshire Boulevard," Eddie added. "If it's too tough for you to figure out, you can give him a call."

"Who are those kids?" Hank Crandall, the water truck driver, asked. "Did they rope you into fixing their washer?"

"I didn't get roped into anything," Zack said, hoping the guys bought his story. "They just mentioned their laundry room is flooded. And I agreed to take a look. That's all."

"Where's their old man?" Hank asked.

"Dead."

"And their mom?"

What was this, the third degree?

"At work. She's a nice lady, and if I can fix the damn thing and save her a couple of bucks on the repair, I don't mind helping out."

"Ohhh…" Dan said, drawing out the response sagely. "I get it."

"Get what?" Zack asked.

A couple of guys laughed.

"What's their mom look like?" Eddie asked.

"Just like a regular mother," Zack lied. "You know what I mean."

"No. Suppose you tell us," Eddie said, with a chuckle.

Oh, for cripes sake. "She's got plain brown hair—not too long, not too short. And she's about average in height. Nothing to shout about." Zack took a long swig of lemonade, then screwed on the lid.

Hell, what was he supposed to tell the guys? That Diana's hair was the shade of honey in the sunlight? That her eyes glimmered like emeralds? That she had a dynamite shape and a smile that could knock the breath right out of a man?

Yeah. Right. He'd never live that down.

He wrapped up the rest of his sandwich, tossed it into his insulated lunchbox and headed back to his dozer.

His days had passed a hell of a lot better when he'd been working alone.

At 12:10, Diana sat before the computer screen in the church office, typing out a letter for Reverend Morton. She planned to break for lunch as soon as she was able to secure his signature, address an envelope and attach a stamp.

The knob turned, the door swung open and Martha Ashton walked in. "Why, hello, Diana. I thought you'd be at lunch already."

"I'll eat in a few minutes. I need to finish what I'm

doing, so I can get this in the outgoing mail before the postal worker arrives."

"I brought in the deposit slip for this week's offering," Martha said. "It was a little on the low side. But then again, it's summer and a lot of the congregation are on vacation."

The telephone rang, and Diana answered, "Park Avenue Community Church."

"Mrs. Lynch, it's me, Megan."

The baby-sitter.

Diana gripped the receiver a little tighter than necessary. "Is everything all right?"

"Yes and no. I was trying to wash a pair of my pants, since I'm going to meet my friends at the mall after you get here and didn't have time to do it before I left home. And then the stupid washer sprang a leak and flooded out the laundry room. I shut it off, but gosh, my jeans are so wet, they'll probably never dry."

Megan's jeans were the least of Diana's concerns. How was she ever going to get by without a washing machine until she could afford a repairman?

"Becky and Jessie went outside and asked that construction guy if he knew anything about washing machines. You know, that tall, dark hottie who drives the bulldozer and fixed your car?"

Yes, she knew who the girls had asked.

Zack.

"Yeah, well, he told them he'd come over after work and look at it," the teenager said.

"I wish they hadn't asked him to do that," Diana said.

"Want me to tell him not to bother?"

Yes and no. Diana was uneasy around the man. Not in a bad way, mind you. But in an I'd-rather-not-deal-with-the-hormones way.

Yet she needed to get the washer repaired.

"Don't bother telling him anything, Megan. I'll take off early today. Maybe I can get it fixed before he gets there." She'd learned to replace the valve in the toilet tank and to unstop the sink. She supposed she could give the washer a try. She just hoped she wouldn't need to buy a new one. Her budget would only stretch so far, and she'd rather go to church in her worn flannel nightgown and slippers than have to swallow her pride and ask her dad for help.

"I cleaned up the water," the sitter added.

"Thank you, Megan."

"And I put my jeans in the dryer, although it's going to take forever. They're sopping wet."

"Try adding a couple of towels to help the dryer work more efficiently," she suggested.

"Okay."

Diana blew out a weary sigh. "Listen, Megan. I've got to get back to work. I'll talk to you when I get home."

When Diana hung up the phone, Martha eased closer. "What was that all about? Did something go on the blink again?"

"The washer is leaking." Diana sat back in her

chair. "I guess Zack, the guy who runs the bulldozer on the construction site, is going to come look at it after work."

Martha furrowed her brow and crossed her arms. "I don't think that's a good idea. There's something about that man—in spite of his good looks. And even though I can't put my finger on what it is, it's unsettling."

Martha Ashton, with her vivid imagination, ought to try her hand at writing a novel.

Yet even Diana had to acknowledge that Zack had a wariness about him. A hardness. Like Travis, the Texas bad boy who'd nearly led her astray.

But Zack had a gentle side, too. She'd seen it. And so had the girls.

"You can't judge a person by his or her appearance, Martha."

"You're too trusting, dear. I worry about you, what with trying to raise those kids alone. And with no husband to look out for you."

Once upon a time, Diana had learned the hard way that having a man around the house didn't guarantee happiness.

Over the past thirty years of her life, she'd gone from being someone's daughter to someone's wife. And somehow, along the way, she'd nearly lost her own identity. Her freedom. Her sense of worth.

And when push came to shove, she'd learned that it was best to only depend upon herself.

So finding another husband was at the bottom of

her list of priorities, right after scrubbing the toilet with a brand-new toothbrush.

"I'm perfectly happy without a man in my life, Martha. After I get the bulk of my work done today, I'm going to ask Reverend Morton if I can leave early. Then I'll go home and take a look at that washer. If I can get it running again, I'll thank Zack for his offer to fix it and send him on his way. Then I'll sit the girls down and ask them not to run to him each time there's a problem at the house."

"It's just so sad," Martha said. "A pretty young woman like you should have a man in her life. That way, you wouldn't have to work outside the home."

"I'm happy to be single. Truly." Diana flashed her a sincere smile. "Now, if you don't mind, I'd better get back to work, especially if I want to take off early today."

But she wasn't able to leave the office until three forty-five. And by the time she pulled onto Shady Lane, there was an old Camaro parked in front of her house. Once a popular and sporty car, three decades had left it in need of a makeover.

And apparently, that's what the owner had in mind. There'd been some bodywork done. And splotches of gray primer had been splashed on to what appeared to be the original black paint.

Was that Zack's car?

If so, it bore a rough edge, too—just like he did.

And just like Travis had, those many years ago.

In spite of her best intentions, a sense of unwelcome anticipation settled over her, and her heart rate slipped into overdrive.

Martha's warning came to mind, and Diana's internal radar began to bleep and buzz out a warning.

But not out of fear of Zack.

Instead, it was her own visceral response that had her concerned.

Damn. The temptation alone was enough to make a preacher cuss and run for the hills.

But before she could gather her thoughts, Becky opened the door and stepped onto the porch.

"Good news, Mom! Zack fixed the washing machine. Shouldn't we invite him to dinner again?"

Chapter Five

Oh, good grief.

Zack had already fixed the washer.

And Becky had practically invited him to dinner.

There wasn't any way Diana could gracefully tap dance around those two facts, so she trudged up the steps and entered the house. She hadn't gotten both feet inside, when Zack came into the living room, as big and gorgeous as you please, a crooked smile pasted on his face that made a single dimple in his cheek.

"I wasn't sure if I could fix it or not," he said, blue eyes twinkling. "But it was a slam dunk."

"It was?"

"Yep." His rebel smile shot straight to her heart,

triggering a wacky disturbance in the course of her already zooming pulse.

"That's good news." And it was, although if truth be told, it seemed as though it had been a long time since things had gone right in her world.

"Come on. I'll show you, just in case it happens again." He turned and walked through the small dining room, into the kitchen and out to the laundry room.

Diana followed, unable to do much of anything else, except marvel at his size, his broad back.

Dark hair, long and a bit unruly, curled at the nape of his neck. It was clean. Shiny. And, she suspected, soft to the touch.

"You see that?" He pointed behind the washer to a black hose that was inserted into a pipe in the wall. "That's how it drains. But for some reason, the hose had come loose, so when the water was pumped out, it went all over the floor."

"You mean there's nothing wrong with the washing machine itself?" she asked, fingers mentally crossed.

"Not that I can tell."

"That's a relief." She sent him an appreciative grin, while trying to still the flutter of butterflies in her stomach. "Thanks for taking time to look at it."

"No problem."

As they stood transfixed in the dinky room, the appliances seemed to disappear, leaving just a man, a woman and a flurry of pheromones bebopping through the air.

Sexual awareness, at least on her part, was enough to take her breath away.

She found it difficult to think of a response, without her mind taking off in all kinds of crazy directions. And her thoughts weren't the only things straying. She couldn't seem to keep her gaze from wandering the length of him.

How tall was he, anyway?

Six foot five or six?

He had an athlete's build—like a professional football player. For a moment, her thoughts took her back in time, when a spellbound teenage girl climbed on the back of a motorcycle, holding on tight to the bad boy who'd offered to take her on a wild ride.

A trip that had been a big mistake.

Her gaze locked on Zack's, yet she didn't speak, didn't move.

She didn't know what kind of man he was. Just because he held that same kind of blood-racing appeal that Travis once had didn't mean their characters were the same.

Zack crossed his arms, biceps flexing and stretching the sleeves of his T-shirt. He stood there, his gaze zeroed in on hers.

Why wasn't he moving?

Oh, for Pete's sake. She was blocking the doorway. What did she expect him to do, pick her up and bodily move her out of the way?

"Well," she said, wiping her hands against her

hips and stepping aside. "I don't know how to thank you for coming to our rescue. Again."

He shrugged, tossing her another lopsided, single-dimpled grin.

"Can Zack stay for dinner?" Becky asked from the doorway.

"Of course," Diana said, trying to regroup. "We're not having anything fancy, Zack. Just a casserole. But you're welcome to join us."

"Reconnecting that hose was no big deal," he said. "You don't owe me anything, let alone another meal."

"We don't mind at all," Becky said. "It gets pretty boring with just the three of us sitting at the table."

Before Diana could think of a response, Megan eased in front of Becky. She had on a snug pair of hip-hugging jeans and a skimpy, lime-green blouse that revealed a silver ring in her belly button that hadn't been there before. At least, Diana hadn't noticed it.

"Is that a new outfit?" she asked the teen.

"Yeah. I got it for my birthday." She glanced down at her pants, then looked up and grinned. "Cool, huh?"

"Wow," Becky said. "You've got a belly button ring. I never saw that before."

Megan shrugged. "I got it pierced a while back. All my friends have them."

Diana knew teenagers did that sort of thing, but Megan's parents were pretty conservative. And notoriously strict. It seemed an odd thing for them to agree to, even though a lot of other parents wouldn't mind.

Had they agreed?

"Well," Megan said, nodding toward the living area of the house. "I've got to go. I'll see you tomorrow."

"Thanks for looking after the girls," Diana said.

"No problem." Megan smiled, then turned and walked away.

Something didn't sit well about the way the young teen was dressed, the way she hurried off.

"What's the matter?" Zack asked.

"I don't know." Diana walked out of the laundry room, through the kitchen and into the living room. She glanced through the screen door, but couldn't see the teenager, who, by that time, had practically vanished.

How was Megan getting to the mall? Who was she meeting? Did her parents know?

Diana turned to find Zack had followed her. So had Becky. But for some reason, her gaze sought Zack's and connected with the only other adult in the house.

"What's up?" he asked, obviously sensing her concern.

"Megan sure disappeared quickly."

"That's because she's going to meet some friends at the mall," Becky said, as though that explained it all. "And she doesn't want to be late."

But Diana knew kids weren't always truthful with adults. And she knew dishonesty often led to disaster. "Becky, where's your sister?"

"She's playing in our room."

"Why don't you two wash up for dinner. Then you can set the patio table."

"Okay," Becky said as she took off down the hall.

Diana looked at Zack. "Is it just me?"

"What do you mean?"

"Megan's parents are pretty strict. And I have this feeling that they don't know what she's up to."

"My old man never knew where I was going or what I was up to," Zack said. "But that's because he never really gave a damn. I guess that's not always the case."

No, it wasn't. Diana's father *had* given a damn. Too much of one, sometimes, even though she'd always tried her best to please him.

But that hadn't stopped her from rebelling one night and going out with a guy who nearly screwed up her young and, up until then, untarnished life.

"If you'll give me a minute," she told Zack, "I'll stick the casserole in the oven. Then, maybe we can sit on the patio and wait for it to heat up. I spend my days in an office, so I love being outdoors whenever possible."

"You sure it's no trouble if I join you?"

She smiled. "On Sunday afternoons, I prepare a couple of casseroles that I can warm up during the week when I don't feel like cooking. So, if you don't mind tuna, it's no problem at all."

But that wasn't entirely true.

For a woman intent on creating a happy, wholesome, single-parent home, she found her daughters' *friend* far more attractive than she cared to admit—especially when she knew nothing about him.

But maybe Zack wasn't anything like Travis. Not in character and temperament. After all, Zack had gotten her car started. And he'd solved her washing machine dilemma. He'd also been kind to the girls.

She supposed it wouldn't hurt to ask him a few questions, to get to know him—as a friend, of course.

Yet she was drawn to him in a more-than-friendly way, mesmerized by a don't-mess-with-me glimmer in his eyes and a bad-boy grin.

And *that,* experience told her, ought to make him off limits.

While the casserole baked, the aroma of tuna and noodles filled the small kitchen, wafted through the screen slider and out to the patio, where Zack and Diana sat outdoors, sipping iced tea.

Earlier, the girls had set the table, then excused themselves to watch a cartoon movie on the Disney Channel.

Zack wasn't sure why he'd agreed to stay and eat with Diana and the kids, especially when he'd planned to steer clear of them. But something about the attractive widow stirred more than just his blood.

"How long have you lived in Bayside?" he asked.

"A couple of months." She slid him a smile. "How about you?"

"I've lived in the San Diego area my whole life."

Other than a five-year stretch of time he'd rather forget, of course. "But I just moved to an apartment in Bayside a few months ago."

"I like this town. It's close enough to San Diego to have the convenience of a big city, yet small enough to feel as though you know your neighbors."

Yeah, well, she didn't know the *real* Zack Henderson. And even though he'd like to open up and be honest, he couldn't see the point. Diana was way too nice for a guy like him. She worked at a church, for cripes sake. And she was the widow of a preacher. She certainly wasn't the kind of woman who'd want to date an ex-con.

Zack didn't always make quick assessments of a person's character, but in this case, he couldn't help it. In his gut, he knew Diana was everything a woman ought to be and he was charmed by her sweet smile, her soft voice.

"Do you have any family around here?" he asked, even though harboring any hope of a relationship with someone like her was a joke. But that didn't quell his curiosity.

"I have a father and a brother in Texas, but it's just the girls and me here."

"It must get lonely," he said, which was an odd thing for him to assume. But a woman like her ought to have a man to share her life.

Her bed.

Ah, hell. Why couldn't he keep his mind from imagining sexual stuff when it came to her?

"The girls are my life," she told him. "I'm content and doing all right."

He figured she probably was.

"What about you?" she asked. "Do you have family around here?"

How much did he want to reveal? That he had a dad who was living under a bridge somewhere, unless he'd drank himself to death? That his mother died giving birth to him because she hadn't had any prenatal care and paramedics hadn't been able to stabilize her?

That he had a daughter someone else was raising because he'd gotten himself in a jam and had spent five years in prison?

He didn't want to go into any of that, but he couldn't very well lie to her. It went against the vow he'd made to stay on the straight and narrow. But he didn't have to toss out too much for her to handle at one time.

"I have a grandmother who's in an assisted living facility. And I have a four-year-old daughter."

At the mention of his little girl, she sat up and smiled. "What's her name?"

"Emily."

"Who's looking after her?"

"Her mom." That wasn't a lie, he told himself. Technically, Caitlin was a foster parent. But she was also the only mother his daughter had ever known. So for all intents and purposes, Caitlin *was* Emily's mom.

"Are you divorced?" she asked.

Shit. This was getting too deep. Too hairy. And honesty was getting tougher to deal with.

But damn it. He wasn't going to lie, even if he had to withhold information she wouldn't understand.

Wouldn't approve of.

"No. I was never married to Emily's mother."

She fiddled with the napkin in front of her, picking at the edges.

Had he surprised her? Offended her?

Well, hell. He couldn't see any reason why he should soften the truth.

There hadn't been much to the relationship he and Teresa had shared. They'd just been two lonely people who'd found a certain comfort and acceptance in each other's arms. They hadn't been in love, so he wasn't sure if he would have married her, even if he hadn't been incarcerated when he'd found out she was pregnant with Emily. But he damn sure would have provided for her. For both of them.

"Tell me about her," Diana said.

"About who?" *Emily's biological mother?*

They might have been lovers, but Zack hadn't known her very well—certainly not as well as he should have, considering he'd gotten her pregnant.

Diana chuckled softly. "About your daughter, silly."

Oh. That was easy.

A grin tugged at his lips as pride filled his chest. "Emily's about as cute as they come. And she loves animals. All kinds of animals. In fact, just yesterday, she asked for a pony."

Diana placed her elbows on the table and leaned forward, as though they had something in common. "My daughters have been begging for a puppy, and I've been waffling. What did you tell Emily?"

"That I live in an apartment. And that a pony needed a large yard." A chuckle of his own slipped out. "She, of course, reminded me that I plan to buy a house with a big backyard someday."

"When are you going to do that?"

When he'd socked enough money away for a down payment.

When his parole was up.

When his life was his own again.

He shrugged. "I don't know. It's a couple of years away."

From inside the house, a timer went off, notifying Diana that the casserole was done. She stood, and Zack did, too.

He wasn't sure about manners and etiquette. Weren't gentlemen supposed to stand when a woman entered or left the room?

The fact he didn't have a clue only made him realize how much he lacked when it came to being around a lady like Diana.

Rather than place the hot baking dish on the glass-topped patio table, Diana prepared the plates in the kitchen, then carried them outside.

Like the last time they'd eaten together, Zack had helped the girls light the candle.

They ate with little comment, other than Becky saying that she and her sister were in a hurry to get back to their cartoon movie. Before long, Diana and Zack were left alone, with a silvery moon and flickering candlelight lending a romantic ambiance.

Every now and again, she slid a peek at the man who sat across from her. Sometimes she caught him glancing away. Had he been trying to steal a look at her, too?

If she didn't know better, she'd think he might be interested in her. But she was a woman with a lot of baggage. Isn't that what bachelors thought about single mothers?

Of course, Zack had a child of his own, something that suggested she'd misread his rebel side.

On the other hand, he hadn't married his daughter's mother.

Diana wasn't sure why that thought brought Martha Ashton to mind like some kind of overactive conscience. Maybe because Martha would undoubtedly find fault with an unmarried man and woman who'd slept together and created a child.

But Diana certainly couldn't. Not when her first baby had entered the world seven months after she and Peter had married.

She might strive for perfection, but she, better than anyone, knew how far she fell short.

Her attention returned to her dinner guest, a man who continued to intrigue her. She wondered if he'd ever owned a motorcycle, if he'd ever gotten suspended from school for smoking. If he'd ever turned a good girl's head.

Then she chastised her imagination and lack of manners.

"Can I get you something else, Travis? More iced tea? Maybe ice cream for dessert?"

"Travis?" he asked, a rebellious grin tweaking only one side of his mouth. "My name is Zack."

Mortified, she tried to regroup. To recover. "I'm sorry. I know your name. I really do. It's just that you remind me of someone I once knew."

"Oh, yeah?" His smile remained lopsided, and the glint of a tease lingered in his eyes. "Who's that?"

"Just a guy I went to school with." She shrugged, hoping to change the subject. To get back to mundane, dinnertime chatter.

"An old boyfriend?" he asked, like a stray dog who'd grabbed onto a meaty T-bone and wasn't about to let go.

"I wouldn't exactly call him a boyfriend."

Travis had been more of a mistake, she supposed. A bad decision. A glimpse into a life of trouble.

"What would you call him?" he asked.

She pushed her plate aside, eager to change the subject. But she wasn't sure how to do so gracefully.

"Not a boyfriend or a date. I never really went out with anyone while I was in school."

"Why not? The boys had to have been crazy not to chase after you."

They would have been even crazier to walk up to the front porch and knock on her door.

"There were a few boys who were interested, but my father was pretty strict. Most guys knew better than to come around, especially when he was home. And I managed to discourage those who were braver than the rest."

"What about your mom?" he asked. "Couldn't she go to bat for you?"

"My mom left home when I was pretty young. So it was just my dad, my brother and me."

By the time she was nine, she'd taken on the role of household nurturer by looking after her younger brother, cooking and cleaning, efforts that never seemed to be good enough. Of course, just because her dad was nitpicky didn't mean he didn't love his little family. He did his part, too, by working his tail off to keep a roof overhead, food in the pantry and the bills paid.

"I can't say that I blame your father for being protective," Zack said. "I'll bet my daughter is going to grow up every bit as pretty as you did. And I won't let just any guy take her out on a date. Not when I know how adolescent boys think."

When it came to being a protective father who distrusted guys with an interest in his daughter, Diana's dad had been worse than the norm. But she didn't say anything.

She also let Zack's comment about her being pretty drop, even though it made her heart swell more than was wise.

Diana didn't feel so pretty anymore. Not after her marriage to Peter.

"I can't believe you didn't date much," Zack said.

She shrugged and admitted, "I rebelled once."

"You?" He grinned. "I find that hard to believe."

"Most people never knew about it. And thank God, my father never found out."

Zack leaned back in his seat, his legs stretching out in front of him. "They say confession is good for the soul."

"Oh, yeah?" She glanced at the sliding door, making sure her daughters were out of sight. Out of hearing range. And when she was satisfied the conversation was private, she told Zack something she'd never told anyone before. "His name was Travis Dayton, and he thought he was about as smart and cool as they came. He smoked, drank, rode a motorcycle and didn't take no for an answer."

"And you found him attractive?" Zack seemed to sit up straighter, egging her on. Daring her to tell the truth.

"There was something dangerous and compelling about Travis, something I found appealing. And one night, while my dad was on a long haul, leaving me and my brother alone, I snuck out of the house to meet him."

Zack arched a brow, yet didn't speak. Didn't ask.

The truth was, things had gotten a little out of hand, in part because of the beer she and Travis had drank. But she wouldn't tell Zack that. She didn't want him to think she'd been a wild child because, other than that one night, she'd always been responsible, dependable and obedient.

Or did she have a rebellious side? Like the one her father swore her runaway mother had? At times, Diana had been afraid it was true. But that was a fear she refused to ponder.

"So you kissed the guy," Zack said. "Didn't you?"

"What makes you think that?"

"If I'd have been Travis, I'd have wanted a kiss. And I'd have figured out a way to encourage one."

Yeah, well, she'd wanted to kiss Travis, too, so encouraging her hadn't been necessary.

Zack studied her with an intensity that sent her blood racing and her imagination soaring. She thought about the heated kisses she'd shared with Travis. And God help her, the memory only made her wonder what kissing Zack would be like.

As good or better, she suspected.

"Then what happened?" he asked.

"We didn't go all the way, if that's what you mean."

Gosh, she couldn't believe she was having this conversation with a virtual stranger. But this particular stranger triggered a lot of the same feelings that Travis had. Only now, she was dealing with them on a grown-up level.

"I got a little scared," she admitted. "And I tried to pull away. But he was really strong, and for a moment, I was afraid he wouldn't stop, even though I'd asked him to."

Zack tensed, and his expression sobered. "I'm not sure why you think I remind you of that guy. He was a jerk. And a fool."

She could understand him taking offense. "I'm sorry. It was just your dark hair and the way you smile that reminded me of him. That's all."

His expression, while still intense, lightened a bit. "Did he finally back off?"

"Yes, but he was really angry." She blew out a ragged, memory-laden sigh. "I always suspected he stopped because a police car had driven up with its red lights flashing, and he was afraid I'd scream for help."

And as happy and relieved as she'd been to see that officer arrive, she'd also been mortified. She'd quickly adjusted her bra and straightened her blouse.

"Did the cop take you home?" Zack asked.

"No, but he followed us to my house."

"Did your dad ever find out?"

"No, *thank God*. He would have killed me. And Travis, too."

"Did you ever go out with that guy again?"

"No way. When the police officer drove off, Travis

tried to talk me into partying with him and a couple of friends at a pool hall on the outskirts of town."

"Did you go?"

She shook her head. "No. By that time, I was afraid of him. And I was so disappointed that the evening hadn't turned out the way I'd expected, that he hadn't turned out to be the hero I'd imagined, I refused to go."

"It pissed him off, didn't it?"

"How did you know?"

"Some guys don't know how to treat a lady."

Did Zack know how?

Something told her he did. And so did his resentment at being compared to a teenage hoodlum.

"Before he left, Travis swore at me again and called me a little tease—among other things. Then he tore off on that motorcycle like the demons of hell were on his tail."

She'd never forget the way his rear tire had spun, as he sped away from her house, leaving her in the dust.

"You were lucky to be rid of him."

She nodded in total agreement. "The next day I found out that while he and his buddies were at the pool hall, they'd gotten involved in a drunken brawl that turned violent. Travis was later convicted and sentenced to six months in jail."

Zack tensed again, and his eye twitched.

Had he found fault with her teenage rebellion? Peter would have, which is why she'd never told him.

But the fact that Zack might have judged her hurt in a way she hadn't expected.

For a young woman who'd never been in trouble before, Diana realized how close she'd come to ruining her reputation and possibly her life.

"For weeks I walked on eggshells, afraid my father would find out I'd been with Travis, that I could have been at the pool hall when the fight broke out." She blew out a shaky breath. "My dad was pretty demanding, even when I toed the mark. He would have completely blown his top if he'd learned what I'd done."

"You didn't do anything wrong," Zack said, as though he understood her need to absolve herself of the guilt she still carried.

"I snuck out of the house when I should have been watching my brother. I kissed a guy who didn't respect me. And for goodness sake, if that policeman hadn't shown up…"

But the officer *had* arrived in the nick of time, thank God. And for some reason—a whole lot of prayer and some divine intervention, most likely— her father had never found out.

"After that, I swore never to get involved with a guy like that again. And I didn't."

It had been a vow that had led to her marriage to Peter—another disappointment that left her feeling guilty. But that was a story she wouldn't go into.

"So there you have it. My guilty secret is out." She

pushed her chair away from the table, stood and began picking up the dishes.

"Here, let me help." Zack reached for a glass and his hand brushed against hers. A shimmy of heat surged though his bloodstream, kicking his heart into overdrive.

Diana must have felt something, too, because she froze, her gaze locking on his. Something strong—and intimidating—passed between them. Something they had no business messing around with.

If she knew that he'd been a guy just like Travis—a hard-ass who'd landed in prison—would she be feeling the same attraction?

Of course, unlike Travis, Zack would have respected her. He wouldn't have laughed and called her a tease, just because she'd had a flash of conscience and a change of heart.

Nope. Even in his hell-bent, hormone-charged adolescence, he would have respected a girl like her.

She ran her tongue along the bottom of her lip—a nervous gesture, no doubt.

Did she have any idea how sexy it was? How it taunted him to touch her? To shove aside his common sense and what few manners he had and press her for a kiss?

His attraction soared into the danger zone, in spite of him knowing better, of knowing she deserved so much more than an ex-con like him.

Just how much of a rebel was he?

Or, better yet, how rehabilitated was he?

Let it go, Henderson.

Walk away.

Laugh it off.

But in spite of a spark of conscience, he lifted a hand and cupped her jaw. Brushed his thumb across the soft skin of her cheek. "Travis was a fool, Diana. He didn't have any idea what he held in the palm of his hand. What he could have had."

She reached up and placed her fingers on his knuckles, as though holding on to his touch. "Thank you. But I was the fool."

"You have nothing to be ashamed of, nothing to feel guilty about. Everyone makes mistakes, especially teenagers." Then he brushed a kiss upon her cheek. "Thanks for dinner."

He slowly lowered his hand and took a step back, making damn sure she remained out of reach. Yet her faint, feminine scent lingered for a moment, before disappearing in the night air.

"You're welcome," she said, her voice whisper soft.

Then he turned and walked away, leaving their plates on the table, leaving her on the patio.

It might not have been the polite thing to do—getting the hell out of Mayberry—but it had been the safest.

And the smartest.

Chapter Six

Long after the dishes had been done and the girls had gone to sleep, Diana lay alone in a double bed that had never before seemed so empty.

The old-fashioned alarm clock tick-tocked on the bureau, reminding her that morning was closing in on her, and she hadn't slept a wink.

She rolled to the side, taking the blanket with her, then she plumped the pillow again. But she couldn't seem to find a comfortable spot to rest her head.

Moonlight peered through the slats of the mini-blinds, illuminating the undisturbed side of the bed. For some stupid reason, she tugged at the spread, pulling it away from the unused pillow as though she weren't lying all alone.

Now how dumb had that been? In the morning, it would take more time to make the bed.

She grumbled, then rolled toward the nightstand and the edge of the mattress. And away from the pillow that no one had slept on since she'd moved into the completely furnished house.

Then she kicked at the covers in frustration.

She knew what was bothering her, what was making it so difficult to drift into a peaceful slumber.

It was Zack and that kiss they'd almost shared earlier this evening.

She wasn't sure exactly what had happened between them, out on the patio and away from the rest of the world. She'd told him something she'd never told anyone—not even her husband. And that brief moment of intimacy had forged some kind of bond between them.

When he'd cupped her cheek and gazed at her, she could have sworn he was going to kiss her.

But he hadn't, and she'd almost been disappointed. *Almost?*

Who was she trying to kid? She *had* been disappointed. And to make matters worse, she couldn't help wondering why he'd held back.

Was he afraid of getting involved with a single mom?

That was possible.

Maybe he was afraid of commitment—not that

she wanted one, mind you. But by his own admission, he hadn't married the woman who'd had his child.

She climbed out of bed, flipped on the light and made her way to the kitchen for a glass of water.

It really didn't matter why he hadn't kissed her. He'd actually done her a favor. After all, she didn't need to complicate her life by entering into an awkward relationship with a stranger.

And Zack probably had his own reasons for not taking a step like that.

She pulled a glass from the cupboard, then turned on the faucet and watched the water run from the spigot to the sink and down the drain.

So why couldn't she let the issue rest? Why not just close her eyes and go to sleep?

Maybe because she feared the dreams that would surely come, if she let down her guard.

Dreams of Zack's smile, his touch.

And of a kiss that almost was.

By the time the rest of the Bayside Construction crew began working at Mariposa Glen, Becky and Jessie had approached Zack daily during lunch, offering him peanuts, raisins, cookies or whatever. Then they would come up with one reason or another for him to stop by after work.

And each time, the guys razzed him.

Zack had thought about eating lunch in his car,

away from the men he worked with, yet he couldn't bring himself to ignore the girls.

More than once, he wondered whether they'd actually been sabotaging things at their house. After all, how the hell could they have accidentally flushed a fuzzy slipper down the toilet?

Most of the time he'd tried to get out of the house or yard before Diana arrived home. It was the only way he could think of to avoid making dinner a habit, especially since the girls seemed compelled to keep feeding him.

So then why, at a quarter to six on a Tuesday morning, was he standing on Diana's porch holding a brown paper grocery bag in the crook of his arm and ringing the bell?

For a moment, he had second thoughts. He briefly considered leaving the sack on the porch and taking off, but that would be the coward's way out. So he shifted his weight to one leg and waited.

She answered the door, wearing a faded blue robe and sleep-tousled hair. Her lips parted, and her breath caught.

"I, uh—" Ah, hell. He dragged a hand through his hair. "I didn't mean to wake you."

Didn't she have to go to work? Hadn't her alarm gone off yet?

"That's all right. I need to get up." She tried to smile, but a yawn caught her off guard.

She looked heart-stoppingly sweet and so damn

appealing. More so in flannel and chenille than in the prim and proper clothing she wore to work. And he realized raw attraction was at work here. Something that made her appear real. Attainable.

He handed her the bag. "Here. This is for you."

"What is it?"

A care package, he guessed. "A pot roast, a pound of hamburger, a loaf of bread. A package of chocolate chip cookies. Snacks for the girls."

"I don't understand." She held the sack in front of her, like a shield of some kind.

"It's to repay you for fixing me dinner the past few nights."

"This isn't necessary. Really."

"Yeah, it is. I'm not a mooch."

She glanced at the bag again, then looked up at him with those emerald eyes. "I can't take this."

"You're going to have to. I can't keep it in my car all day long." He flashed her a crooked grin. "It'll rot."

She tucked a strand of hair behind her ear, leaving him a glimpse of a long, slender neck made for nuzzling and kissing.

It hadn't been a good idea to come here. But he paid his own way. He always had.

She peered inside the bag. "Oh, my gosh. That pot roast is big enough to feed an army."

"Maybe you can cut it in two and freeze part of it?"

"No, I'll just ask Megan to throw it in the oven this

afternoon. That way, it will be ready about the time you and I get off work."

"That's not why I brought it to you."

She slid him a pretty smile. "I'll be home about four-thirty this evening."

That *really* hadn't been his intention. He was skating around those awkward dinners. But he couldn't seem to come up with a reason why he shouldn't accept the invitation—one she'd made without the girls prompting her.

Then an idea struck. One that meant she wouldn't have to cook for him.

"Why don't you save the roast for another time. I'll come by after work and take you guys to Burger Bob's instead."

She fiddled with the frayed lapel of her robe, her fingers delicate, nails unpolished but filed neatly. Her expressive gaze nearly turned him inside out and shook the stuffing out of him. "You don't have to do that."

"I know. But the girls might enjoy getting out and doing something different."

My…budget is a bit tight right now." She offered him a wistful smile. "Maybe next week?"

"This is my treat. I owe you, remember?"

She glanced at the bag of groceries. "I thought this was the payback."

He shrugged. "That and a couple of hamburgers at Bob's. What do you say?"

"What time do you want to go?"

"How about six?" That would give him time to shower and change clothes. She'd never seen him when he wasn't dirty and dusty.

And for some dumb reason, what she saw mattered.

It had been ages since Diana had stewed over what to wear anywhere, let alone a burger place that catered to families with children. But stew was what she'd done from the moment she'd gotten home from work.

At a quarter to six, she finally settled on a pair of blue jeans and a white cotton blouse. This wasn't a date, for goodness sake.

She slipped into the pants, realizing they were a bit tighter than she remembered. She wasn't sure why she'd bought them during that closeout sale. Maybe because they made her feel pretty.

They fit stylishly snug and low at the hips. If she were a younger woman on the prowl, it wouldn't be a problem, but now, as she prepared to face Zack, a case of buyer's remorse settled over her. Oh, she still felt pretty when she glanced into the mirror, but she also felt sexy, which is why she almost changed her mind about wearing the jeans.

Then she scolded herself for being so self-conscious. It wasn't as though she and Zack were going somewhere alone. They were taking the girls to a fast-food restaurant, for goodness sake, a come-as-you-are sort of place.

But as she put on the blouse, her fingers stumbled

with the buttons. Should she leave the top couple un-done? It actually looked better that way. More casual. More relaxed.

She dressed pretty conservatively for work. But this was different. What would it hurt to let her hair down, now that she was off the clock?

And speaking of hair, she'd fussed with that, too, sweeping it up, which had seemed too sophisticated. Then she'd pulled it into a ponytail, which was too young and playful. So she'd finally decided to let it hang loose on her shoulders—like a typical soccer mom might.

The girls had been thrilled that Zack had invited them to Burger Bob's. But not just because going out, even for fast food, was a real treat. Or because the burger joint had a big, colorful indoor climbing structure.

For some reason, they were especially excited about riding in Zack's car. The old Camaro didn't look much better than Diana's Plymouth on the out-side. And even though it was considered a vintage model, she doubted that the girls saw the value in that.

Maybe they merely thought the world of Zack.

"Mom, he's here!" Becky called from the living room.

"I'll be out in a minute," Diana responded, before glancing one last time in the bathroom mirror and swiping her finger against a black speckle of mascara that rested under her eye.

Then she grabbed the bottle of pear-and-melon lotion from the counter, nearly knocking it into the sink.

She scolded herself for being so nervous. Tonight was no big deal. Just burgers and fries. A low-key outing with the kids, that's all. And that's all she wanted it to be.

So why on earth did it feel like a date?

She quickly squeezed a dollop of the creamy lotion into her hands and rubbed it into her skin. After taking a deep, calming breath, she left the bathroom and headed for the living room, where she spotted Zack before he caught sight of her.

He wore a pair of black jeans and a gray T-shirt—both looked new. His hair was still damp from the shower.

When he realized she'd entered the room, he shot her a one-dimpled grin that sent her heart cartwheeling through her chest.

His gaze caressed her, as a warm glimmer in his eyes suggested that he appreciated her efforts to find just the right thing to wear.

Had he dressed with her in mind, too? She couldn't help wishing he had, as crazy as *that* was.

She ran her moist hands—from the lotion she'd used, and surely not from nerves—over her denim-clad hips. For a moment, a sexually charged silence settled over them. Or over her, anyway.

"Hey." His square-cut jaw bobbed up in a greeting. "You sure look nice in that."

Pride and nerves tangled in her throat, making it difficult to respond without falling all over herself and acting goofy.

"Thanks." She glanced down at her pants. "It's just a pair of jeans."

"They look great."

Somehow, she got the feeling he was talking about the fit. And she had a sudden urge to run back to her room and put on a pair of sweatpants. She hadn't *meant* to dress in a way that would entice him. Well, not so that he'd suspect she'd done it on purpose.

"Thanks for taking us to dinner tonight," Becky said, relieving some of Diana's self-inflicted pressure. "Jessie and I love Burger Bob's."

"That's what I figured," Zack told the girl.

"I'm *really, really* hungry," Jessie said. "When do we get to go?"

"If it's okay with your mom," Zack said, turning his attention back to Diana, "we can go now. I've been craving Bob's Triple Beef and Bacon Burger all day."

"That's fine with me." Diana reached for her purse and took out the keys. After they'd all stepped onto the porch and her daughters skipped along the sidewalk toward Zack's car, she locked the house.

Zack stood by the passenger door, holding it open for her. And the fact that he'd done so nearly brought tears to her eyes. No one, not even Peter—back when they'd first dated—had done something so thoughtful, so polite.

She slid into the car, and when he'd made sure her legs were in, he closed the door.

"Hey," Becky said, when Zack climbed into the driver's seat. "Whose baby car seat is back here?"

"It's my daughter's," Zack said. "I forgot it was back there."

"You have a baby daughter?" Jessie asked, brown eyes growing wide. "I didn't know that."

Diana realized, in all the times he'd chatted with her girls, he hadn't told them about Emily. And she wondered why.

"Yes, I have a little girl. But she's not really a baby anymore, even though she's still required to sit in a car seat. She's four. And just starting preschool this week."

"Is she going to Burger Bob's with us?" Jessie asked.

"No, not today."

"Then next time?"

Zack tightened his grip on the steering wheel and started the engine. He didn't turn around, didn't look at Jessie through the rearview mirror. "Maybe so. We'll have to see."

That was pretty noncommittal, Diana realized. Was he taking it slow and easy? Just getting his feet wet?

Or maybe the offer of dinner at the hamburger place was just what he'd said it was—a way of re-paying Diana and the girls for providing him dinner a couple of times.

The rest of the drive was relatively quiet. And be-fore long, they'd pulled into Burger Bob's parking lot, gotten out of the car and entered the fast-food restaurant with an indoor climbing structure that would keep the girls entertained for hours.

"Can we play first?" Jessie asked. "Please. I'm not hungry yet."

"You said you were back at the house," her sister reminded her.

"But I changed my mind. Maybe, if I get to play for awhile, my stomach will be hungry again."

"Do you mind if we wait a little bit before ordering?" Diana asked Zack. "Or are you in a hurry?"

He cracked a smile. "I don't think anyone with kids ever expects to make a quick stop at a place like this. Why don't we sit down and let them play. I'll get us something to drink."

"Okay."

"How about a chocolate shake?"

"I probably ought to have a diet soda," she said, realizing how hard she had to work to keep her weight from zooming out of control, especially with all the starchy food that didn't put too big of a crunch on her budget.

"But you like chocolate," he said, blue eyes boasting a boyish glimmer.

Yes, she did. "It sounds tempting."

And so was his smile. In fact, the man would tempt a saint.

"You don't have to drink the whole thing."

She'd never invested in anything she didn't intend

to use. But he made it difficult to be frugal. Or wise. "All right. I'll indulge, but just for tonight."

At least, when it came to having a calorie-laden shake. Would there be other temptations, as the evening wore on?

He flashed her a smile that made her want to treat herself to more than chocolate.

"Why don't you find us a table," he suggested, "while I place the order."

"Sure."

Minutes later, Diana sat on a red-vinyl seat in a corner booth, her hands resting on the white Formica tabletop. Every once in a while, she spotted one of the girls crawling through a section of the bright yellow tunnels suspended overhead.

As Zack approached with a tray of drinks, she smiled at him. "The girls sure love this place."

"I figured they would. Emily enjoys it so much that she and I come here almost every Sunday afternoon." He placed the tray on the table, then unloaded four shakes, a king-size order of fries and several plastic pouches of ketchup.

She arched an eyebrow. "I thought you were just getting a couple of milkshakes."

He shrugged. "I thought the girls might be happy with a snack."

"This is a snack?" She nodded toward the appetite-stealing shakes and fries.

"Yep. Especially when I can eat two of those Triple Beef Burgers with bacon and cheese and still feel hungry." He tossed her a playful grin. "Would it make you feel better to call it an appetizer?"

Oh, what the heck. She tried her best to make nutritious snacks and meals for her daughters. What would it hurt to let down her guard for one night?

"We'll call it whatever you like." She reached for a fry and popped it into her mouth.

Zack couldn't help watching Diana eat and was mesmerized by the way her lips parted as she slid a fry into her mouth, the way her jaw moved slowly, seductively. By the way she swallowed.

She had one of those swanlike necks made for kissing, and he couldn't help wondering what kind of throaty noises she'd make, if he…

Nah. He wouldn't do something that bold. Not in a public place, anyway. Or even in private, he supposed.

Ever since that night on her back porch, when he'd nearly kissed her, he'd made a point of keeping his hands to himself. After all, she'd vowed not to get involved with anyone like that hard-assed rebel she'd snuck out with as a teenager.

And even though Zack could list a hundred ways he was different from and better than Travis Whatever-His-Name-Was, the bastard who hadn't appreciated her, one truth came busting to the forefront.

Diana deserved more than Zack could give her.

Yet here they sat, like two teenagers out on a Saturday afternoon date. He grinned at the irony.

Years ago, he'd never brought a girl to a place like this. His idea of a date had been sharing a bottle of cheap, fruity wine—the kind with a screw-top lid—while stretched out under the camper shell that covered the bed of his truck. And unlike that jerk Travis, Zack hadn't had any trouble finding a nice, quiet place, away from prying eyes.

Or from police officers who drove by looking for minors making out.

He glanced at Diana, saw her watching him. What was she thinking? Had she picked up on the romantic vibes he'd been getting?

Probably not at a place like this. Not with all the noise and clatter from the kitchen or the kids shrieking as they slid down purple tubular slides or crawled through yellow plastic tunnels.

So why was he finding this place hormone-stirring?

Okay. So it wasn't the setting at all. It was the woman sitting across from him. And he was getting a testosterone buzz just by watching her.

But moments later, when Becky and Jessie came running to the table, out of breath, their hairlines damp with perspiration, the image of anything remotely datelike vanished.

While Zack placed their dinner order, Diana took Becky and Jessie to the restroom to wash up.

Their burgers and chicken strips were up in no

time at all. And before long, the girls had eaten their fill and taken off to play again, leaving Zack and Diana alone once more.

"Thank you for bringing us here," she told him. "The girls are having a good time. We haven't gotten out much this summer."

"I'm glad this is a treat for them."

For a moment, he thought about the barbecue he'd been invited to at Harry Logan's next weekend. He'd only attended a couple of the functions Kay and Harry had hosted. But each one had been fun, making him feel like one of the guys who'd been dubbed Logan's Heroes, a group of one-time juvenile delinquents who'd turned their lives around.

Harry had planned an informal badminton game. And there'd be plenty of food, not to mention the camaraderie of the guys Zack was beginning to think of as brothers.

He wondered whether he should invite Diana and the girls—just as friends, of course.

Sometimes one of the guys brought a guest, who'd always been welcome.

An invitation was on the tip of Zack's tongue, yet he held back. Would she misunderstand his intention?

Hell, he knew better than to get involved with her—romantically speaking. So maybe, if he worded it just right…

"You know, since you mentioned that you and the girls haven't gotten out very much this summer, I thought you might like to go to a barbecue with me on Saturday. A friend of mine and his wife, who have become surrogate parents to me, always put on a nice spread. And I'm sure they wouldn't mind if I brought you and the girls as guests."

She seemed to be seriously considering the invitation, then she scrunched her face. "It sounds really nice, but I'd feel funny tagging along to a party."

"Believe me, it's not a party. It's more of a get-together. And if it makes you feel better, I'll call and get an okay from them first. But I can pretty much guarantee they'll say, 'The more the merrier.'"

"You're sure?"

"Absolutely." He shot her what he hoped was a disarming smile.

"If it's okay with them, and if you don't mind, I suppose it would be fun to go to a backyard barbecue. Can I bring something?"

"How about some of those oatmeal cookies?"

"That's all?"

"You can make a double batch, if that makes you feel better." Zack tossed her a smile. He'd also pick up some extra hot dogs, buns and soda.

"All right," she said, releasing a pretty smile that sent his senses topsy-turvy. "It sounds fun."

Zack sat back in his seat, proud of himself for asking her. And happy she'd agreed to go.

But on the way home, after dropping her and the

girls off at their house, he realized he might have been a bit premature with the invitation.

After all, there was a good chance that since Brett was one of Logan's Heroes, too, that he, Caitlin and Emily would be there.

And as much as Zack would love to see his little girl on a day other than Sunday, he realized Diana was going to need an explanation about Emily's living situation.

What would Diana think when she learned Zack's four-year-old daughter lived in foster care and not with him?

Or that Zack didn't allow Emily to visit him at his place, not when he had to worry about his probation officer showing up unexpectedly for a random search—something that might frighten and confuse her, since that kind of thing would never happen at her house.

Would the subject of his five-year stint in prison come to light? And if so, what would she think of him then?

He'd been convicted of a crime he'd witnessed, yet hadn't committed. But early on he'd learned that most people believed the worst about an ex-con. And in the past, Zack had decided to not even give a rip.

But damn. He was going to look like a big loser in Diana's eyes.

And that hurt more than he cared to admit.

Chapter Seven

There'd been seven whole days during which Zack could have leveled with Diana. But each time he'd driven past her street, each time he'd picked up the phone to call, he'd chickened out.

So that left Saturday afternoon—the day of the barbecue.

By the time he got to her house, a Boy Scout couldn't have tied his stomach in a tighter knot. He parked his car at the curb, then plodded up the walk.

Why had he set himself up for this?

Why hadn't he given more thought to inviting her and the girls to go with him today?

Well, it was too damn late to backpedal now. He

was committed; his course was set. So he lifted his hand and knocked lightly on the door.

The girls greeted him with an enthusiastic welcome that nearly bowled him over.

"Hi, Zack! We're ready to go."

"Mommy made cookies, and we helped."

"Are there going to be kids there?"

"Can I take my soccer ball and jump rope?"

"Slow down," Diana said, as she carried a platter filled high with cookies out of the kitchen and into the living room. "You're not even giving Zack a chance to respond."

"That's okay," he told her. "They're just excited." But his focus wasn't on the girls and their eagerness, but rather on Diana.

She wore a simple white sundress, and her sun-kissed brown hair had been swept into a twist held by a big, black clip.

"The girls have been making plans about what to wear and what to take since the moment they woke up this morning." She slid him an angelic smile he didn't deserve.

Zack made a halfhearted attempt to return a grin, trying to act as though everything was just fine, as though he wasn't filled with dread about telling her something that would shade the way she looked at him from now on.

But it didn't seem to be working.

"What's the matter?" Diana asked, obviously picking up on his reluctance to speak, to move.

"Nothing. But I was wondering if...before we go...I could talk to you alone."

"Sure." She placed the platter of cookies on the coffee table. "Girls, why don't you go into your room and find something to do for a few minutes."

As Becky and Jessie grumbled and trudged down the hall, Zack shoved his hands in the pockets of his jeans.

"Do you want to talk outside? Maybe on the back porch?"

He nodded. "Yeah. Sure. Outside is good."

During his time at Riverview—a place that had neither a view nor a river running anywhere near it—fresh air and sunshine had become luxuries. So he figured being outdoors, especially since he'd had to earn the freedom to be there, would make telling her what she needed to know easier.

"Can I get you a cup of coffee or a glass of iced tea?"

He would really like a stiff drink about now— whisky, straight up, ought to do it—but he slowly shook his head. "No, thanks. I'm fine."

She led him out to the patio, where they took a seat.

"What's wrong?"

Zack sucked in a deep breath, unsure of how to start. How much to reveal. And when he gazed into Diana's eyes and saw compassion and understanding—something he might never get from her again—

he wanted to bolt across the yard, leap the block wall onto the construction site and hightail it home.

But he didn't.

He cleared his throat, trying to dislodge his nervousness, his reluctance. "My…uh…daughter might be at the barbecue, and there's something I need to tell you about her before we go."

Diana's breath caught. Was there something wrong with Zack's daughter?

Was that why he hadn't talked to the girls about her?

Back in Texas, Diana had worked as a bookkeeper at Buckaroo Ranch, which had originally been a resort for the rich and sometimes famous, until Jake Meredith, her friend and boss, converted the fancy dude ranch into a camp for handicapped children. With the help of his wife, Maggie, who was a top-notch pediatrician, Jake and a qualified staff provided the kids a safe environment in which to play.

What Zack didn't know was that Becky and Jessie had spent a lot of time at the ranch, playing with the children, many of whom had cerebral palsy, like Kayla Meredith.

Her daughters had always been kind and accepting of people who were different, so she had every reason to believe they would do just fine with his little girl.

"I'm sure Becky and Jessie will enjoy meeting and playing with Emily. Don't worry." She reached across the table and took Zack's hand in a move meant to make his revelation easier and to let him know she understood. But as her fingers grazed his scarred knuckles, a flood of warmth rushed through her veins, triggering more than her sympathy.

She tried her best to ignore it, to rally her senses, until his pained expression turned her heart on end, releasing a flurry of emotions too tender to explore.

"I'm sure you're right. The girls will get along great." His voice came out husky and deep, as though his reservations weighed it down.

"Then what do you have to explain?" she asked.

"Emily's real mother died on the day she was born. And when the hospital released Emily, she was sent to live with a foster mother."

"And?" Diana asked, knowing there was more to his story than that.

"She still lives there." Zack took another deep breath, as though he needed the oxygen to clear his head. As though he was struggling with the reason his daughter lived in foster care and not with him.

"You don't have custody?" She wondered if that was by choice.

"No. When I was a teenager, I got into a lot of trouble."

Diana merely nodded, letting him know she'd heard him, even if she didn't quite understand.

"When Emily was born, I was doing time for a crime I didn't commit."

Her eyes widened, and her lips parted. He'd been in jail? Or was it juvenile hall? He said he was inno-

Get **FREE BOOKS** and a **FREE GIFT** when you play the...

LAS VEGAS
GAME

*Just scratch off
the gold box with a coin.
Then check below to see
the gifts you get!* →

YES! I have scratched off the gold box. Please send me my **2 FREE BOOKS** and **gift for which I qualify**. I understand that I am under no obligation to purchase any books as explained on the back of this card.

335 SDL D7ZH   235 SDL D7Y7

| |
FIRST NAME   LAST NAME

ADDRESS

APT.#   CITY

STATE/PROV.   ZIP/POSTAL CODE   (S-SE-06/05)

7	**7**	**7**	Worth TWO FREE BOOKS plus a BONUS Mystery Gift!
🍒	🍒	🍒	Worth TWO FREE BOOKS!
🔔	🔔	☘	TRY AGAIN!

www.eHarlequin.com

BUSINESS REPLY MAIL
FIRST-CLASS MAIL   PERMIT NO. 717-003   BUFFALO, NY

POSTAGE WILL BE PAID BY ADDRESSEE

SILHOUETTE READER SERVICE
3010 WALDEN AVE
PO BOX 1867
BUFFALO NY 14240-9952

NO POSTAGE
NECESSARY
IF MAILED
IN THE
UNITED STATES

cent, but what had he been charged with? How long did he have to spend behind bars?

Before she could quiz him, he seemed to gloss over the incarceration. "Emily's real mom, Teresa Carmichael, was a young woman I'd dated for a while. We weren't in love with each other, and I doubt that given time, anything like that would have developed."

He looked at her as though wanting her understanding, or maybe even her absolution, yet she just sat there, quietly taking it all in. If anyone had less of a right to sit in on a confession about premarital sex, it was Diana.

"After my arraignment, Teresa came to see me and told me she was pregnant. There wasn't much I could do about it at that point. My hands were tied...or I guess you could say they were cuffed."

"How did Teresa die?"

"When she was eight months pregnant, she was waiting at a bus stop, on her way to serve a Thanksgiving meal down at a rescue mission near the border. And during a drive-by shooting, a stray bullet struck her in the head. She was in a coma by the time they got her to the hospital. And before she died, Emily was delivered by caesarian, then placed in foster care."

"Didn't either of you have family that could have taken the baby?"

"Teresa never talked about her family or the reason why she ran away from home as a teenager. And since my Uncle Hank wasn't able to look after an infant, the courts placed Emily with Caitlin."

Diana couldn't seem to think of a response, and he must have sensed her…surprise…confusion… concern.

"You have to understand," he said, his eyes pleading. "Caitlin is a loving woman and the only mother my daughter has ever known. I couldn't take her away from the kind of home I'd always wished I'd had. When you meet the Tanners, you'll understand why."

Diana tried to smile, as though she understood already. But she couldn't imagine letting someone else raise her daughters. And she didn't know why Zack didn't fight to have more time with his child.

Was there even more to the story than he'd told her?

"Emily means the world to me," Zack explained. "And I'm trying my hardest to be the kind of man my daughter can look up to."

"I'm glad to hear that," Diana said. "Why was it so important for you to tell me that now? Before the barbecue at your friends' house?"

"Because Emily and her foster parents will probably be there. And because we've been honest with Emily. If she should mention something to you or the girls, I wanted you to understand the agreement I made with the Tanners, why I made it and, more importantly, why I'm abiding by it."

"I see."

"Are you okay with it?" he asked.

She conjured a smile. "I'm not the one who has to be okay with it. You, Emily and the Tanners are."

He nodded. "We're all in agreement."

"Good."

"So, now that we've got that out in the open," he said, "do you still want to go?"

Not really. Diana didn't understand why, after four years, he still didn't at least have joint custody of his daughter. But her biggest worry was about the trouble Zack had gotten into as a teenager. And her concern about the kind of people he hung around with, the friends who were hosting the barbecue.

Martha Ashton's voice popped into her head like a Jack-in-the-box with a bad spring, shaking a finger and triggering a rush of concern.

There's something about that man—in spite of his good looks.

Was there? Had Martha seen something in Zack that Diana had missed?

…even though I can't put my finger on what it is, it's unsettling.

Quite frankly, Diana felt a little uneasy, too.

You're too trusting, dear. I worry about you, what with trying to raise those kids alone. And with no husband to look out for you.

Had Diana been naive? Should she be skeptical?

She hated to quiz him about the trouble he'd been in four or five years ago, so she opted to ask him about his friends.

"I just realized you haven't told me anything about our hosts." And if she decided to go to their house, she wanted to know something about them.

"I can't believe I skipped over that. Harry and Kay Logan are about the nicest people you'll ever meet. In fact, they're practically famous for their hospitality."

"Kay Logan?" Diana asked. "Is she a redhead? Petite and in her late-fifties?"

"Yeah. Do you know her?"

"I think so. Did her husband have open heart surgery last winter?"

"Yes, he did. It sounds like you *do* know them, but that's not surprising. Harry is a retired detective and Kay is pretty active in the community. How did you meet them?"

"It's not as though we're actually friends, but I met her at the church office where I work. The entire congregation knows who Kay is and talks very highly of her and her husband." For that reason alone, Diana felt a whole lot better about going with Zack and meeting his friends.

"The Logans are the best," he said. "And I'm glad they've welcomed me into the fold."

That was good enough for Diana. So she pushed her chair away from the table and stood. "I'll go get the girls."

And as Zack followed her back into the house, she chased Martha's voice from her mind, hoping the small echoes would die down and leave her in peace.

* * *

For the most part, the adults rode in silence to the Logans' house. But that didn't mean they didn't respond to the girls' many questions.

"Will there be any other kids at the barbecue?" Jessie asked.

"There's usually at least one or two. My daughter, Emily, might even be there. Her mom had other plans today, but thought they would be able to come by a little later."

"That's good," Becky said.

Zack parked along the curb on Bayside Drive, in front of a white, Cape Cod-style home. They exited the car, then made their way up the sidewalk of a well-manicured yard and stood before a floral welcome mat at the front door.

Moments later, Kay Logan answered and smiled warmly at Zack. Then, when she recognized Diana and the girls, she brightened.

"Well, this is a lovely surprise. Zack said he was bringing guests, but I had no idea it would be the new church secretary and her daughters." Kay embraced Diana, taking care not to knock the platter from her hands. "I'm so glad you're here. Please come in."

"I hope you can use an extra dessert," Diana said. "I wanted to bring something, and Zack suggested cookies."

"That's perfect. We're expecting a couple of children today. But then again, most of the guys who'll be here are really just big kids at heart."

Kay took the platter from Diana. "Harry and Luke are in the backyard, Zack. Why don't you take the young ladies out to get a soda or juice from the ice chest on the patio."

Zack took the girls outside, while Kay led Diana through a cozy living room and into a kitchen that was painted pale lavender and bore a wallpaper trim of small violet bouquets. A myriad of appliances sat upon white countertops, indicating that Kay Logan enjoyed cooking.

"You have a nice home," Diana commented. "And with a kitchen made for entertaining."

"Thank you." Kay grinned, her cheeks blushing with pride. "Harry and I love to have the kids come home. And I don't mean just the ones I gave birth to. We've practically adopted a dozen or more young men along the way. Zack's one of the more recent."

As Kay placed the cookies on the counter, next to a chocolate layer cake and an apple pie, Diana glanced at the breakfast nook. A round, antique oak table and four chairs sat near a big bay window that was framed by an Irish lace valance.

She imagined Kay and Harry having their morning coffee at the table, looking out into a backyard filled with plants, ferns and palm trees—each one trimmed neatly.

On the patio, a built-in barbeque grill sat amidst

redwood furniture. A badminton net was stretched across the lawn.

Zack, Harry and a man she didn't know had set down their drinks and were showing the girls how to hold the racquets and where to hit the birdies to make them soar over the net.

"How did you meet Zack?" Kay asked.

Diana turned away from the window. "He's working on the construction site behind our house. And the girls met him first. I'm afraid they've been asking him to make various household repairs while I'm at work and then inviting him to stay for dinner."

"Zack's had a rough time of it," Kay said. "I'm glad to know things are going well for him now. Have you met his daughter yet?"

"No, I haven't."

"She's a darling little girl. You'll get to see her today. Brett and Caitlin are bringing her by a little later."

"Zack talks highly of Caitlin," she said. "I'm looking forward to meeting her."

"Caitlin is a wonderful woman and mother. When you meet her, you'll know what I mean. She used to be a nurse at Oceana General, but now that she and Brett are married, she's been able to stay at home with Emily."

"That's nice." Diana wished she could stay home with her daughters, but that was impossible.

"Teresa, Emily's biological mother, would have

been happy to know that her baby was given to a woman who loves her as her very own."

"Zack said Teresa was killed while waiting at a bus stop."

"Yes, she was. It was so tragic, so senseless. Teresa was becoming a real success story for Lydia House."

Diana knew that Lydia House provided shelter for young women who'd found themselves on the street. Just recently, the organization had received an award from the mayor, recognizing their positive influence upon the community.

If Diana had more time, she'd love to get involved with the shelter, but as it was, she was pedaling as fast as she could, just to be able to work and find quality time with the girls.

"Unfortunately," Kay said, "no one has ever been charged in the shooting."

"That's too bad."

And ironic, too. Whoever had killed Emily's mom had gotten away scot-free. And her father, if Zack had been telling the truth, had been punished for a crime he hadn't committed.

Before Diana could figure out a polite way to get a little more information about Zack's conviction out of her hostess, Kay suggested they go outside and join the others.

That was just as well. There would be other times to talk to Kay, to quiz her about Zack. Diana would do her best to enjoy the day, the company and the hospitality of one of the nicest couples in Bayside.

As Diana stepped onto the patio, her gaze landed on Zack, on the pair of worn jeans he wore, the clean white T-shirt with a surfboard shop logo. He appeared relaxed here, at home. Yet when his gaze met hers, his movements stilled, causing the people and voices to drift and fade and placing the two of them on some unseen plane.

A growing sense of sexual awareness nearly knocked the breath out of her, in spite of the presence of others.

She tried to regain control of herself, of her interest in Zack. But whatever was buzzing between them was making it difficult.

And she sensed that he was feeling it, too.

Zack had been watching Harry show Jessie how to swing the badminton racquet when the screen on the sliding door swooshed open. As Kay led Diana into the yard, like an angel who'd stopped by for a cup of tea—or whatever it was that they shared with mortals—his heart skipped a couple of beats.

The bridal-white sundress boasted her purity, her innocence. And when she smiled…

Zack's heart lodged in his throat. A man would be damn lucky to have a woman like her on his arm, in his life.

He watched as Kay introduced her to Luke Wynters, another one of Logan's Heroes who'd pulled his life out of the gutter and gotten a scholarship to college and later medical school. Zack's life hadn't taken that big of an upward swing. But then again, Luke had allowed Harry into his life at an earlier age, and Zack had been a hell of a lot more stubborn.

Diana extended her arm and shook hands with Luke. "It's nice to meet you."

Luke, who wore a sober and clinical expression a lot of the time, broke into a warm grin. "The pleasure is mine."

Zack's pulse sounded like a hollow thud in his ears, and a sudden fist of jealousy caught his throat in a death grip.

What the hell had he done?

Of all the single guys who'd become part of the Logan clan, Luke was the one who deserved a woman like Diana. And it damn near made Zack sick to his stomach to think he'd brought her here, hoping she'd like his friends.

He sure as heck hadn't meant to set her up with the good-looking, fair-haired, single doctor.

Before he could curse his stupidity or figure out a way to stop the ache in his chest from getting any worse, the doorbell rang.

And, bit by bit, the Logans' home filled with happy voices and laughter.

Diana was introduced to several of the guys, including Nate Barlow, who was nervously awaiting the results of the bar exam, and T.J. Montoya, who'd just landed a job with the Bayside police department.

Her warm smiles and friendly greetings suggested she was accepting his friends.

Was she accepting Zack, too?

Had she realized he'd put his life back on track, like all the other men here?

He hoped so, more than he cared to admit.

When Joe and Kristin Davenport arrived, along with their son Bobby, the girls, who apparently didn't have a shy bone in their bodies, challenged the boy to a game of badminton. Harry piped up, saying it was a great idea. Moments later, they'd chosen teams and the game was on.

Zack's nervousness slowly dissipated, as he coached the girls and encouraged a competitive streak in little Jessie that he hadn't seen before.

But as Diana carried two empty glasses into the house, the doorbell sounded from within, announcing another arrival.

Zack's belly knotted again. This time, he figured it had to be the Tanners.

Would Diana understand why he hadn't fought for custody of his child?

For some reason, everything he'd battled long and hard to achieve seemed to hang in the balance.

Chapter Eight

Diana stood at the sink, rinsing out two glasses, as Kay entered the kitchen with an attractive couple and a cute little girl.

"I'm sorry we're late," the woman said. "But Brett's son has been attending a summer camp through the city parks and rec department, and they wrapped up the program with a big three-sport tournament between the kids."

"Don't be sorry," Kay told the couple. "I'm so glad you're having the opportunity to be involved in Justin's life, even when it's not your weekend to have him."

"So are we." The blonde tucked a golden strand of hair behind her ear, revealing a pearl earring. "I brought a Waldorf salad. Can I put it in the fridge until it's time to eat?"

"Of course. Harry has just started the grill, so it won't be long." Kay turned toward the sink, where Diana stood. "Caitlin and Brett, I'd like to introduce you to Diana Lynch. She's the new secretary at Park Avenue Community Church. And she's also a friend of Zack's."

Caitlin reached out a hand to Diana. "It's nice to meet you."

Brett, a handsome man with dark hair and blue eyes, followed his wife's lead and extended his arm in the customary greeting. "How do you do?"

A scar over his right brow indicated he'd been in a tussle or two, but that was the only outward sign that he might have been one of the teenage trouble-makers Harry had reached out to.

"I've been looking forward to meeting you," Diana said. "Zack talks highly of you both."

"Do you know my other daddy?" Emily asked, with dancing blue eyes the same shade as Zack's.

Her mom, Diana presumed, had pulled back the sides of her long, blond hair with rainbow-colored barrettes and dressed her in a white, puffy-sleeved blouse, green-gingham shorts and a pair of brand-new white tennies.

Zack hadn't been biased when he told her about his daughter. She was a darling little girl who appeared to be loved and well cared for.

Diana smiled at the child. "Yes, Emily. I *do* know your other daddy."

"Where is he?" the blond pixie asked. "I saw his car outside."

"He's on the patio," Kay said. "Come along. I'll show you. And then I'll introduce you to a couple of little girls who would love to play with you."

Kay led Emily outdoors, leaving Diana a little nervous about making small talk with Caitlin and Brett Tanner—maybe because she feared they might be sizing her up, the way she was doing to them.

"Zack mentioned he'd met a woman and her two daughters," Caitlin said. "How long have you been dating?"

"We're not dating," Diana said. "Not really. We're just friends."

"Oh, gosh. I'm sorry for jumping to conclusions." Caitlin flushed but recovered quickly with a gentle smile. "Brett and I have been hoping Zack would find someone special. But a good friend is nice to have, too."

The old adage said you couldn't judge a book by its cover, but it didn't take Diana long to decide that Caitlin Tanner was everything Zack had said she would be.

As Kay entered through the open sliding door and strode toward the kitchen, the telephone rang.

"Hello?" She smiled broadly. "Hi, honey. We thought you'd be here by now." Then her brow knit, and she frowned. "When? Did you call the doctor?"

Diana couldn't hear the other side of the conversation, but she easily concluded that it wasn't good news.

"Don't worry, sweetheart. Your father and I will be right there." When Kay hung up the phone, she said, "That was our daughter, Hailey. She's a little more than eight months pregnant, and her water broke. Her husband, Nick, is on a stakeout, so Harry and I need to take her to the hospital."

Caitlin placed a hand on Kay's shoulder. "Don't worry about leaving. Brett and I will make sure everyone eats. And then we'll clean up."

"I'll be glad to help, too," Diana said. "Please go be with your daughter."

"Thank you," Kay said, before dashing outside to find her husband.

Moments later, as Harry grabbed his keys from a rack with small hooks near the telephone, Kristin Davenport, who'd been outside watching the children play badminton, entered the kitchen. She placed a hand on her own distended womb and addressed the older couple. "Please give Hailey our best. And don't worry about anything at the house. Joe and I will wait here until you get back."

Harry fiddled with his keys, removing one from the ring and handed it to Kristin. "Thanks, but I hate to have you feel stranded here. Stay as long as you like and lock up if you need to go."

"Give us a call when you can," Kristin said.

"I will, but…" Concern etched across Kay's maternal face. "It's a little early for her to be having the baby, so I hope everything goes all right."

Caitlin slipped an arm around Kay's shoulders. "I can understand your worry, but it shouldn't be a problem. She's got a great obstetrician, and the staff at Oceana is the best. I'm sure she will be just fine."

Dr. Luke Wynters, who'd just come in from the backyard, agreed. "I was going to cut out early this afternoon, since I'm on duty tonight. But I'll head over to the hospital now. Nick doesn't get ruffled easy, but fatherhood just might do it. And I'm going to be the first to raz him."

Brett chuckled. "Nick will be a heck of a dad, once that baby gets here. But he's been the classic expectant father. From what I understand, he's been calling Hailey every half hour, just to check on her."

Harry, who'd pulled out a camera from the coat closet in the living room, winked at Brett. "We'll have to watch and see what kind of expectant father you make, son."

Brett slipped an arm around Caitlin and drew her close. "I'll probably be worse."

Just as Zack had told her, the Tanners seemed like a loving and likable couple. And after the first flutter of nerves upon meeting them, Diana found them both easy to talk to.

The afternoon progressed smoothly, even without Harry and Kay to supervise and help Diana feel at ease.

The women prepared a buffet table, setting out paper plates, napkins and plastic utensils. Then they began to load it down with salads, chips, condiments, buns and a Crock-Pot filled with beans.

Brett and Joe jumped in to keep the kids entertained, while Zack flipped hot dogs and burgers over the grill.

Diana carried out a clean platter, on which he could place the cooked meat. And although Zack seemed to be diligently watching over the sizzling burgers, his eyes continued to dart toward the children, toward the laughter and play.

A flood of warmth settled in Diana's chest. She may have had concerns before, but after meeting his friends and watching Zack with his own little girl and doing his best to fit in, she felt much better about his influence on her daughters.

Of course, to complicate matters further, her attraction to him was deepening and she couldn't help wondering if maybe she was that "someone special" Caitlin had mentioned Zack needed.

Hanging out with Harry and the guys had always been a pleasant experience, and with each outing or get-together, Zack was made to feel more and more welcome. But this was the first time he'd actually considered himself one of Logan's Heroes. As weird as it sounded, he seemed to really fit in today.

As the afternoon drifted into evening, Kay called home several times, first letting everyone know Hailey had been admitted to the hospital and was in active labor.

The next piece of news revealed that since Hailey was only three weeks early, the obstetrician didn't appear to be worried about either her or the baby. Kay also reported that Nick had finally arrived, looking every bit as haggard and flighty as the nervous expectant father the guys had claimed he'd become.

By the time the kitchen had been cleaned up, the grill had cooled down and all but three couples had gone home, Harry called to say that after a quick and uneventful labor, he and Kay had a brand-new grandson. And, he added, Nick and Hailey had decided to name the six-pound-two-ounce infant Harry Logan Granger.

Joe Davenport, who'd taken that phone call, said the retired detective had actually choked back happy tears.

It had been Joe's idea to pop a bottle of champagne, and Zack wondered whether Diana would have a glass or if she considered alcohol, even in moderation, a vice. After all, his experience with ladies like her was limited.

But interestingly enough, she was the only woman who accepted a flute of the bubbly drink. Kristin Davenport, who was expecting twins, opted for soda. And Caitlin, with a flush to her cheeks, did the same, announcing that she and Brett were having a baby, too.

Wow.

Zack wondered how many little kids would be

running around in the not-so-distant future. And, of those, how many would boast having one form of Harry's name or another.

They all lifted their glasses in a toast to little Harry Granger and his family. As the sound of clinking crystal filled the room, Zack felt as though he had something to celebrate, too, but he'd be damned if he knew exactly what.

The fact that Diana hadn't labeled him a loser?

The fact that she fit right in with the others and somehow validated his true acceptance into the group?

The adults who'd remained at Harry's house—the Davenports, the Tanners, along with Zack and Diana—sat just off the kitchen, in the family room, chatting and laughing about one thing or another. The children, Emily, Diana's daughters and Bobby Davenport, had long since gone into the den to watch the Disney Channel on TV. And while Zack latched on to the glow, the warmth and the easy camaraderie of people who were becoming his friends, his eyes continued to light on Diana, to make sure she was comfortable hanging around when others had already left.

She certainly seemed to be enjoying herself.

But when she finished her champagne, he thought it would be a good idea to offer her the option of leaving.

"Did you want to stay a bit longer?" he asked her. "Or are you ready to go home?"

Home.

If Zack was prone to fantasy, he could almost imagine that he and Diana were a couple, planning to take their daughters to a house they shared and turn in for the night.

"Sure. We probably should. It's getting late." She got up from her seat on Harry's easy chair and headed for the kitchen, where she rinsed her glass in the sink. Then she disappeared down the hall toward the den.

Zack followed her lead, intending to wash out his own glass and set it on the counter.

At the sink, Caitlin sidled up to him and nudged him with her elbow. "Diana says you're just friends."

"That's right," he said.

Caitlin broke into a playful grin. "I'll give that *friendship* about a week."

Zack's gut clenched.

Had Caitlin suspected that Diana was going to break things—or whatever—off with Zack in less than a week?

Well, not that they were dating. Or even seeing each other in *that* sense. But, if he wanted to be honest, especially with himself, he had to admit the thought of something more than friendship with Diana had crossed his mind.

But did Caitlin think the single mom and church secretary was too good for an ex-con?

His gaze pounced on hers like a man overboard

reaching for a life preserver that had been tossed into rough seas. "Why do you say that?"

Caitlin's eyes widened, and her lips parted. "For goodness sake, Zack. You look like someone just kicked your dog."

Well, hell. It felt as though someone had certainly sucker punched him. He had half a notion to shrug off her comment, but something deep inside wouldn't let him. "What makes you think our friendship won't last?"

"Zack," she said, smiling in spite of the seriousness of his question. "I was giving a platonic relationship with her only a week. I've seen the way you look at her, and the way she's been sneaking peeks at you. It's obvious to me, even if you haven't figured it out, that you're both fighting the feeling. And whatever you're tiptoeing around is going to come out on top."

Talk about sucker punches. He was speechless.

Caitlin laughed. "Just look at you."

What was wrong with him? Was it that apparent? That noticeable?

Diana was the nicest, most virtuous woman Zack had ever met. And the prettiest. But he certainly couldn't…well, he wouldn't…

Wait.

Caitlin had said she'd sensed something about Diana's feelings for him, too. She claimed to have spotted a glance, something in Diana's eyes, her expression.

Was she right? Had Zack missed it?

Damn. Women found it so freaking easy to talk about that kind of stuff—relationships, feelings.

But he'd be damned if he'd ask for clarification. Not when he'd sped through that adolescent insecurity stage more than ten years ago.

At least, he sure hoped he had.

Twenty minutes later, he pulled the Camaro along the curb in front of Diana's house.

"Would you like to come in for a cup of coffee or something?" she asked.

Yes.

No.

Ah, shoot. He didn't know what to say, without sounding too eager. Too interested. Too caught up in Caitlin's implication that Diana was feeling something for him, too.

So he took on that cool, what-the-hell attitude that came so damn easy. "Sure. Why not."

He followed her into the house, waiting as she instructed the girls to take a bath and put on their pajamas. Then she led him into the kitchen, where he watched her put on a pot of coffee.

"Thank you for taking me to the barbecue at the Logans'," she said. "We had a great time. And I enjoyed meeting your friends."

"I'm glad you went." He'd always felt a little like a party crasher at Harry's, even though everyone had always been accepting. But he didn't mention a thing to Diana. He didn't flash a glimpse of his underbelly to anyone.

As the coffee brewed, she pulled out milk from the fridge, sugar from the cupboard and two cups. "Why don't you have a seat. I'm going to check on the girls, but I'll be back in a flash."

Then she disappeared, leaving Zack alone in the cozy kitchen.

He glanced at the countertops, spick-and-span, with everything put away neatly. Then he took a seat at a gray and turquoise dinette table that sat in the corner, a bowl of fruit as a centerpiece.

On the wall, a glossy calendar hung, along with one of those wipe-off markers. She had a dental appointment on Thursday. The fifteenth was someone named Mary's birthday. There was an ice-cream social at the church the last Sunday of the month.

He inhaled the aroma of the fresh brew, appreciating the comforting scent, the homey feeling of being in Diana's house in the still of the evening.

Of being her invited guest—not just because the girls had forced the issue.

And he thought about Caitlin's comment, her prophecy of sorts.

I've seen the way you look at her, and the way she's been sneaking peeks at you.

Diana returned to the kitchen, although her steps slowed when she reached the center of the room. She tucked a strand of hair behind her ear, something

Zack noticed that she did often. A nervous habit, he suspected.

Nervous?

Caitlin's words again came to mind. *You're both fighting the feeling.*

As he began to realize that Caitlin might be right, reassurance surged through his chest.

"The kids doing okay?" he asked.

Diana nodded, then slid him a pretty smile. "Yes. They're taking a bath now, and I wanted to make sure they weren't playing around, that they had towels and their pajamas laid out."

Whatever you're tiptoeing around is going to come out on top.

Were they tiptoeing around their feelings?

And would whatever it was grow stronger, becoming hard to ignore? Impossible to resist?

She glanced at the coffeepot on the counter, then back at him. "It's ready."

"Good."

It sure felt as though something was going on between them, something silent yet strong. And he wasn't sure what to do about it. Let it happen?

Or turn and walk away before he got in too deep?

She poured two cups, then handed him one—just the way he liked it, black, hot and freshly brewed.

As she carried it to him, he reached to take it from her. Their eyes met, and something passed between them. Their hands touched, and a warm jolt shivered along his skin, traveling deep inside of him, convincing him that Caitlin had zeroed in on his far-from-platonic thoughts.

Diana felt it too, he suspected, because her eyes widened and her fingers trembled—or had it been his that shook?

Either way, the cup tilted and hot coffee splashed all over his hand.

"Ouch. Damn it." Oh, cripes, he'd let a damn slip out in front of her.

"I'm *so* sorry," she said, clearly aghast.

"No problem."

She set the cup on the table and took his hand in hers. "Are you okay? Here, let's rinse it with cold water."

"It's all right." It would just hurt for a minute, that's all.

"Your skin is red." She drew him to the sink and turned on the water, but her touch, her faint floral scent, her closeness chased the pain away and brought something else into the picture.

"It's okay," he said. "Really." But he let her hold his hand under the flood of cool water.

"Are you sure?" she asked.

It didn't hurt anymore. But that was about the only thing he was sure of. "I'm fine."

She turned off the spigot, then grabbed a folded dish towel from the countertop and carefully blotted his wet hand, drying it.

And all the while, he stood there, stunned. Caught

up in something he didn't understand. His heart thundered like a runaway train, as his blood rushed through his veins, stirring up his libido and laying open his desire.

Her movements stilled, and she glanced up at him, caught him watching her.

Something a hell of a lot stronger than his conscience snaked around his chest and throat, making it hard to breathe, hard to talk.

He'd always tried to mind his manners around her. Tried hard to respect her, to treat her the way a lady ought to be treated.

But the rebel deep in his soul refused to remain dormant any longer.

He pulled his hand free, then cupped her face. His thumb caressed the skin of her cheek.

Her expression grew serious, and her eyes darkened with something he hoped was desire.

When her lips parted in what he decided was an invitation, he threw caution to the wind, lowering his mouth to hers.

The kiss began slowly, gently. Sweetly.

He expected her to pull away, but when she slipped her arms around his neck, drawing him close, deepening the kiss, he knew she'd stopped fighting her apprehension, too.

Their tongues touched, shyly at first, then with a blood-stirring boldness that damn near took his breath away.

She tasted like gumdrops and smelled of roses, and he was soon caught up in a heady, sexual rush, the likes of which he'd never known.

Their hands began to seek, to caress. But before their exploration could really get underway, the sound of footsteps and a child's voice drew them apart.

"Oh, wow," Becky said, her eyes wide and a goofy smile plastered on her face. "Cool."

No, not cool.

Scary.

"I…uh…" Diana glanced at Zack, as though he had something bright and witty to say, something to explain to the precocious, ten-year-old child, something he couldn't even grasp himself.

Zack raked a hand through his hair. "I'm… sorry…for…" Hell, he didn't know what he was even sorry for. Being caught? "Hey, maybe I ought to go home. I've got an early day tomorrow."

"Oh," Diana said. "All right. I probably ought to get to bed early, too."

"Hey, don't mind me," Becky said, with a grin as big as all get-out still plastered to her face. "I'll just go back to my room and read Jessie a bedtime story."

As the child turned her back and trotted off, Diana looked at Zack, her cheeks flushed. "I don't know what to say to her."

"Neither do I." He took a deep breath and slowly blew it out. "I hadn't counted on kissing you. It just sort of happened."

"I know."

"We...uh...well...it doesn't have to mean anything."

She smiled, but something in her eyes said it was too late for that. They'd stepped across some invisible line.

"It was nice, though." He slid her a crooked smile, trying to make light of what they'd done. Trying to coax some kind of confession or explanation from her.

"It was *very* nice." Her voice came out soft, yet husky.

"Maybe we can pretend it didn't happen," he said. "If it makes you feel better."

"I'm not sure what will make me feel better. But pretending it didn't happen won't work. We had a witness, remember?"

He nodded, thinking he understood her confusion, her reluctance to let things go unchecked. He wasn't sure what to make of it either, or what he wanted to make of it. "Maybe we ought to take it one day at a time."

"That sounds like a good idea."

As he started to leave, she grabbed his arm, drawing him back. "Would you like to have dinner with us later this week? Maybe on Wednesday?"

A grin tugged at his lips. "Yeah. I'd like that."

Then he decided to take off.

While he was still ahead.

* * *

On Tuesday evening, after work, Diana stopped at the market to pick up a few things for the dinner she'd planned for Wednesday. She'd actually gotten in and out of the store pretty quickly, but the traffic had been exceptionally bad, and she was eager to get home.

She'd hardly climbed from the car, when Martha Ashton flew out her front door and hurried down the walk with a skip and a waddle.

"Reverend Morton said you left work more than an hour ago, and I've been waiting for you to get home. I have something to tell you."

By the look on her round face, she hadn't won the lottery.

Diana reached for the small grocery bag that sat on the front seat, then closed the car door. "What's the matter?"

Martha glanced over her shoulder, as though ensuring privacy, then leaned forward and lowered her voice. "I saw that construction fellow earlier today. He was working on the faucet in your side yard. You know, the one by the camellias?"

Diana nodded. Apparently, the girls had found another chore for Zack to do, and she couldn't keep the hint of a smile from twitching her lips.

"Well, when I caught sight of his profile, I suddenly realized where I'd seen him before."

Diana juggled her purse and the heavy sack of groceries. The box boy should have placed the items in two bags. "Where did you see Zack?"

"On the front page of the *Bayside Banner*." Martha crossed her arms, a smirk settling across her face.

"In today's paper?" Diana asked.

"No. It was an article that came out about four or five years ago."

"I don't understand," Diana said.

"Let me explain. I stopped by the Speedy Stop this afternoon and saw the article posted behind the register. Apparently, Mr. Tompkins, the owner of the convenience store, keeps it posted as a reminder of the day two young hoodlums ruined his life."

"What happened?"

"Your construction worker, Zachary Henderson, and another young thug robbed the Speedy Stop and shot Mr. Tompkins, the owner. The poor man was paralyzed and remains in a wheelchair to this day."

Diana's heart thumped against her rib cage, threatening to pound its way out of her chest. And her blood cooled to the point of making her head light and her knees weak.

Zack had been involved in a robbery and a shooting?

It seemed impossible to imagine him as a violent criminal. But the thought that she might have misjudged him weighed heavily on her mind.

"Are you sure it was Zack?" she asked, hoping Martha was mistaken.

"I certainly am. And I'm so glad I put two and two together. He's a convicted criminal. And he's been nosing around your place, possibly even staking it out."

"I know that Zack got into trouble as a kid," Diana said, wanting desperately to defend him, yet having a difficult time doing so. She couldn't get over the fact that someone had been shot during a crime he might have been involved in.

"That's putting it mildly. Both of those young men were known juvenile delinquents."

"Zack's trying hard to be a law-abiding citizen," Diana added, although she was unsure whether she was hoping to convince Martha or herself.

"Well, tell that to poor Mr. Tompkins. He used to play Santa Claus down at the boys and girls club each year. And he used to donate many of the toys himself. And now he's crippled."

"I appreciate you telling me," Diana said, as she shuffled the bag again. "And you're right. Having an ex-con hanging around the neighborhood is a concern. But I've come to trust Zack."

"Humph." Martha shook her head slowly. "You have a lot more faith in the criminal justice system than I do."

"I believe in forgiveness and giving people second chances, especially when they're trying to turn their lives around," Diana said, using both hands to steady her load.

"Well, that's all well and good. But I watch a lot of television and read the paper, too. And while I realize we shouldn't be casting stones, I think you ought to be leery about who comes in contact with those sweet little girls of yours."

"I *am* careful," Diana said, hoping that she and Harry Logan were both right about Zack.

"Well, I believe that old saying. Leopards don't change their spots."

"I'll keep that in mind." Diana tried her best to muster a smile. "Thank you for your concern."

Then she headed for the front porch, her stomach clenched into a knot and her heart as heavy as the sack of groceries she carried into the house.

Chapter Nine

Following Martha's revelation, Diana vacillated between confidence and suspicion.

Deep in her heart, she wanted to believe Zack was innocent, that he hadn't been involved in a violent crime. After all, he'd been so sweet, so gentle with the girls. And he'd treated her with the utmost respect.

That evening, she'd gone through the motions of feeding the girls and getting them ready for bed.

But it had taken her hours to fall asleep, only to wake in a cold sweat, with a gunshot echoing in her dream, the shadowed vision of a body slumping to the floor of a convenience store. Bright red seeping through a white, cotton shirt, turning it a haunting shade of crimson.

She'd risen while it was still dark and splashed cold water on her face, trying to chase away her doubts.

Martha could have gotten her facts wrong. Maybe it had been another Zachary who'd been involved in the robbery.

But Zack *had* told Diana he'd gotten into some trouble and hadn't been able to take care of Emily after her birth. Diana had just assumed he'd spent a little time in jail.

But had he been in prison for armed robbery?

It was Wednesday morning.

And she'd invited Zack to dinner tonight.

A part of her wanted to call him and postpone. Or even to cancel altogether. But there would be no way around her uneasiness until she had a chance to talk to him and hear his side of the story.

She was still going through the motions, her heart torn between blind trust and cold doubt.

But as far as she was concerned, there was only one thing to do. She had to learn the truth. And what better way than to confront Zack tonight while they sat across the table from one another.

She prepared a pot roast for this evening and would ask Megan to take the roasting pan out of the fridge and put it into the oven this afternoon so it would be ready when Zack arrived.

And since Diana didn't want the conversation

hampered by the presence of her daughters, she had to figure out a way to get the girls out of the house tonight.

Once at work, she called Eleanor Pringle, an elderly woman who lived on the other side of town and occasionally baby-sat to earn a little spending money to supplement her income from Social Security.

Eleanor said she'd be happy to watch Becky and Jessie, and Diana promised to bring hamburgers for dinner and a child-appropriate video for them to watch that evening.

So when Reverend Morton agreed to let her off work early, the plan was set into motion.

Diana arrived home to the hearty aroma of roast beef—thank goodness Megan hadn't forgotten her instructions. Then she announced that the girls were going to spend the evening with Mrs. Pringle. And since she hadn't told them she'd invited Zack to dinner, they were excited about their evening plans.

So forty-five minutes later, Diana delivered her daughters, a cartoon video, three orders of fries, two kid-sized hamburgers and a double cheeseburger to Mrs. Pringle's house. Then she went home to freshen up, set the table and wait for Zack to arrive.

As the clock ticked steadily, announcing that the time was drawing near, Diana fiddled with the place settings several times and adjusted the simple but pretty centerpiece, a small glass bowl of water that held three pink camellia blossoms.

She fought the urge to run to her bedroom and check her hair and lipstick one more time, especially when she thought about the heady, mind-spinning, knee-buckling kiss they'd shared. A kiss she hoped wouldn't cloud her judgment when it came to gauging Zack's true character tonight.

When the doorbell rang, her heart nearly fluttered out of her chest, and her hands, which were a little too clammy for comfort, had a slight tremble.

She stood straight, brushed her palms along the cotton fabric of a simple black dress, inhaled a deep breath, then slowly let it out as she made her way to the door to allow her guest entrance.

Zack stood on the stoop, blue eyes dancing, a crooked grin tugging the corner of his lips.

He'd shaved. And although he looked about as handsome as a man could be in a pair of neatly pressed khaki slacks and a turquoise and green Hawaiian shirt, she couldn't help missing that rebellious five-o'clock-shadow—just a little.

Realizing that she'd been studying him a bit longer than was polite, she stepped aside and cast him a smile. "Hi."

"Hey." He lifted a bottle he held in his hand. "I brought some red wine, thinking you might like some with dinner."

"That was nice. Come on in." She led him into the living room, aware of his presence, the woodsy scent of his cologne.

Way too aware.

"The girls are sure quiet," he said.

"I…uh…took them to a sitter."

A heavy silence filled the room, as pheromones zipped and zapped between them.

They were alone.

Would he assume she'd done it on purpose to make this evening more romantic? Would he think she wanted to see where the kiss they'd shared last Saturday would lead?

The memory of his lips on hers, tongues seeking, hands caressing, warred with Martha's revelation. It demanded that Diana learn the truth about Zack's alleged crime, to exonerate him and get on with life. To see where the future might lead.

Or to end things before she got in too deep, before she dragged her innocent children into something they didn't deserve.

"I thought," she said, deciding to be direct, "that we had a few things to talk about. And I figured the girls didn't need to hear them."

"You're probably right."

They stood in the center of the living room, guest and hostess. Man and woman. A couple treading upon uncharted ground.

She slipped a loose strand of hair behind her ear. "Dinner's just about ready."

He again lifted the wine. "Would you like to open it before we eat?"

He gripped the neck of the bottle, with a big hand that had once caressed her almost reverently.

A hand that had gripped a gun.

No.

She hadn't misjudged this gentle giant of a man. And she wouldn't give fear free rein.

"Sure, a glass of wine sounds good." Of course, she rarely touched alcohol, but tonight, she suspected it would make broaching the subject she wanted to talk about a little easier. "Come on. There's a corkscrew in one of the drawers in the kitchen."

Zack followed Diana through the small house, his eyes scanning the length of her.

She wore a plain black dress, nothing fancy. Yet he couldn't help watching the way the fabric swished softly against her hips, the way the hem brushed against her shapely legs. Even from behind, she was a beautiful woman.

Once inside the kitchen, she reached into a drawer, pulled out a corkscrew and handed it to him. "I'm afraid I don't drink wine very often. And I'm not familiar with opening a bottle like that. The corkscrew came with the furnished house. So, do you mind doing the honors?"

"No, not at all." Zack wasn't all that familiar with wine, either. Harry had suggested a nice bottle of Merlot, giving Zack the name of several good California wineries.

After fiddling with the darn corkscrew for a moment, not quite sure how it worked and hoping an aptitude in mechanics would help him figure it out, he finally managed to pop the cork.

He turned to see Diana on tiptoes and reaching for the glasses on the highest shelf in the cupboard, the fabric of her dress stretching and tugging at the hem, giving him a quick glimpse of shapely thighs.

"Here," he said, "let me get those for you."

She tossed him an appreciative smile. "Thanks."

Minutes later, he poured them both a glass.

He wondered if he ought to toast her, like he'd seen suave, cocky actors do in the movies a time or two. But he figured he'd botch it up somehow. And rather than risk having her think he was goofy, he just lifted the glass to his lips and took a drink.

The taste of Merlot, he supposed, was something he'd have to get used to. Truthfully, he'd rather have a cold beer.

But dating a woman like Diana—if dating was what they were doing—was new to him. And so was the proper protocol in social situations.

"I've never had red wine before," she said.

Did he dare admit he hadn't either? At least, not the kind that had a real cork and cost more than twenty dollars a bottle.

"What do you think?" he asked her.

"It's kind of nice." She offered him a shy smile, then turned to grab a pair of potholders and removed the roast from the oven.

She seemed nervous, as though she had something heavy weighing on her mind. But whatever it was, she didn't bring it up at dinner. And he didn't ask. After all, he didn't like people probing his mind, prying into his thoughts. Digging up his past.

So they pretty much made small talk while they ate roast beef, potatoes and carrots, commenting about the warm summer they'd been having. About the Padres' winning streak. About the traffic congestion at the merge. But he couldn't help thinking about the things that had been left unsaid over dinner.

"Why don't we go into the living room," she suggested, when they'd finished eating.

"All right."

"I'll just put the plates in the sink and leave them for later. Would you like a bowl of ice cream?"

"No," he said. "Actually, the wine is starting to grow on me. I think I'll have another glass. How about you?"

"Sure."

He picked up the half-empty bottle and both glasses, then carried them into the cozy living room. He poured her a drink, then handed it to her when she returned.

She accepted it and sat on the sofa.

He took a seat on the sofa, too. Not too close, not too far.

God, this was awkward. But kind of nice.

She fingered the stem of her glass, while her eyes

studied the rich, burgundy-colored liquid. Then she glanced across the sofa at him. "Do you mind if I ask you a question?"

Yes. No. "Go ahead."

"You mentioned getting in trouble before Emily was born. And that you weren't able to take care of her."

The dull thud of his heartbeat pounded in his ears, sounding out an omen of some kind. But he wasn't going to tap dance around the truth, not with Diana. "Yeah, I did."

"What kind of trouble did you get into?"

Zack wanted to backpedal, to renege on the permission he'd granted her, to refuse to answer the question she'd wanted to ask. Or at least to soften the blow.

More than anything, he wanted to keep his past from her forever.

All of it.

Every sorry detail that clearly proved why he didn't deserve to have a woman like her as a friend, let alone as a lover.

But if she was going to end things between them before they even got a chance to get started, it was better now than later. Before he invested too much hope into an impossible dream.

So he made an irrevocable decision—one he feared might haunt him in the days to come.

He would own up to what happened, revealing the truth about his past so that there wouldn't be any secrets circling like a vulture, ready to pounce and tear a dying relationship to bits.

He took one last look at her as she sat demurely with that wineglass in her hand, a datelike pose he might never see again.

"I didn't have the kind of childhood you did," he said, thinking that if she knew about the anger and resentment he'd grown up with as a child she might better understand his rebellion, the trouble he'd gotten into.

While behind bars, he'd been forced to look at his past, to account for his actions, to accept his present and plot out a new future.

She turned toward him, watching him with eyes that insisted she deserved to know the truth, that she deserved to map out her own future—with or without him.

"My mother had been a foster kid who'd struck out on her own and hooked up with the wrong crowd, the wrong guy. I don't think she bothered seeing a doctor during her pregnancy, and she developed something called toxemia. She had me two months early." He flashed her what seemed like a wimpy grin. "Hard to believe I only weighed a little over two pounds at birth, huh?"

She returned his smile. "It sounds to me like you were a born survivor."

"Yeah, I guess you could say I came into this world fighting." He'd never looked at it that way. But the chips had been stacked against him from birth. Maybe that's where all that adolescent rebellion had come from.

She continued to watch him, waiting. Listening.

Actually giving a damn, maybe?

"I was born at home, delivered by paramedics, and my mother died from complications that could have been prevented."

"That's too bad," she said.

Too bad that his mom died? Or that she hadn't made her baby's health and well-being a priority?

Both, he guessed.

"When the paramedics told the authorities about the situation at home in the rundown apartment where my mom and dad lived, I was sent to foster care. Well, once I got out of an incubator, that is."

"So you grew up with foster parents?"

"Not for too long. When my dad's mother was located, she took me in. Things were pretty stable and normal for my early years. But when I was six, my old man got married and supposedly straightened out. He'd gone into rehab and wanted to take me back. Then he petitioned the court, who decided, considering my grandma's health was failing, that I should live with him."

"It's tough for children to be uprooted."

"Yeah," he said. "That's one reason why I couldn't do it to Emily, not when I saw how much she and her foster mom loved each other."

Diana nodded, and he hoped that she truly understood. That she realized he'd put his daughter's happiness and well-being above his own. That he didn't want to be the kind of parent he'd had.

"Were you happy living with your father?" she asked.

"At first, it wasn't so bad. But my dad had never really kicked his drug habit. And eventually my stepmother got fed up and moved out. At least, that's the way I saw it."

"I'm sorry," she said.

He didn't want her sympathy, just her understanding. So he shrugged it off. "When my dad hit the skids, my uncle stepped up to the plate."

"What about your grandmother?" she asked. "Couldn't you have gone back to live with her?"

"No. Her arthritis was getting worse. And the court thought a teenager would have been too much for her to handle. And knowing me, they were probably right."

"Was your uncle good to you?"

Zack supposed that would be a mother's concern, that a child was treated well. "He was nice enough and a heck of a hard worker, but every night after quitting time, he'd vegetate in front of the television with a case of beer, leaving me to raise myself."

"Is that when you started getting into trouble?"

"Yeah." The more serious trouble, anyway.

"What about school?"

"I did okay. At least, I managed to get a diploma."

Actually, if Zack had given a damn about academics, he could have aced all of his classes. But he hadn't—other than an auto shop class he'd had. He seemed to have an aptitude for anything mechanical, and it was the one thing that had made him feel halfway good about himself.

"I had plenty of reasons why I should have kept my nose clean. For my sixteenth birthday, my uncle gave me an old pickup that no longer ran. And I began taking apart the engine at night." He slid her a smile he hoped didn't seem too cocky. "I eventually got it running, too."

"That's something to be proud of."

"Maybe so, but it didn't mean that I kept away from the wrong crowd. Or that I didn't roam the city streets after curfew." Zack had always had a rebellious side that his uncle just couldn't seem to tame. Especially when the guy wasn't available on weekends or in the evenings.

"What kind of trouble?"

He leaned forward, placing his hands upon his knees, the scars from a hundred fights still adorning his knuckles. "I was a big kid. And I matured early. So I didn't have any trouble buying booze or being served liquor, even when I was still a teenager." He glanced up at her, gave her a wry grin. "It made me pretty popular in my crowd."

"I imagine it did." Her voice didn't seem to hold any disgust.

Hadn't she made a judgment yet? Well, there was still plenty of time for that.

"One night, a couple of us went into a bar and got a little loud, I guess. But that's about the size of it. Then this ass…I mean, jerk, who was stinking drunk and obnoxious, picked a fight with us. I hit him. A few minutes later, he went down for the count."

"Passed out?" she asked.

Zack watched her expression, saw her eyes widen, and he searched for that disgust. The frown.

She hid it pretty well.

"I didn't kill him, if that's what you're thinking. He had a heart attack."

He again glanced at her face, studying her expression, her demeanor. And although she didn't smile, she didn't curl up her lips in disapproval, either.

"I met Harry Logan that night. He was one of the cops who'd been called to the bar. And for some reason, he took an interest in me. He said I was on a one-way street to trouble, if I didn't start making some changes. Then he talked to my uncle about giving me some guidance."

"Did that help?"

"My uncle and Bob Adams, a neighbor and guy he worked with, got me a summer job picking up sticks and trash while bulldozers were clearing a hillside. And with the money I earned, I bought tools and parts to rebuild my truck engine. In the evenings, Bob helped me with that old pickup. And before long, we got it running."

"It sounds like things started getting better for you."

"Things got worse before they got better. Teresa, the girl I'd been seeing, told me she was pregnant. I wanted to do right by both her and the baby, but what kind of dad or husband would I have made, especially then?"

She didn't respond to his question, and he wasn't sure if that was a good thing or not.

"About that time, Harry stopped by after I got off work and talked to me about life and setting goals. Believe it or not, what he had to say actually made some sense. Then he invited me to play ball in the park near the marina one evening with him and a bunch of the guys."

"Did you go?"

"I'd actually planned to, but things didn't work out that way."

"What happened?"

"On the night of the game, my truck wouldn't start, so I was just going to say screw it about joining Harry at the marina. But an old friend, Ray Montalvo, came by. I should have known better, I guess, since Ray was bad news and Harry had warned me to steer clear of him. But we'd been pretty tight as kids, and I asked him to drop me off." Zack shook his head. "I'm still amazed at the turn of events, at the stupid mistake I made being with the wrong guy at the wrong time."

She didn't speak, she just sat there, her eyes warm,

brow furrowed. Intent on listening, it seemed. On hearing the rest of his confession, words that might drive her away for good. But he couldn't stop now.

"Ray wanted to go by the Speedy Stop first. I smoked back then, so I figured what the heck. I'd run inside and pick up a pack of cigarettes and buy a soda. But what I didn't realize was that Ray had another game plan. One I didn't know anything about."

Zack half expected her to slide closer to the armrest of the sofa, to withdraw. To want to wash her hands of him. But she didn't appear to have moved away at all. In fact, if anything, she seemed to lean to the side. Closer to him.

He took a deep breath, then blew it out. "Ray slipped on a ski mask after I went inside, then he pulled a gun and entered the store. I'm not sure how it all went down, since I was back in the refrigerated section of the store, but a shot was fired. And when the owner came running out with a gun, too, all I could think of doing was ducking for cover."

"You weren't involved," she said, her voice whisper soft.

"No, I wasn't. The cashier got a bullet in the arm, and when the owner turned to look at his wounded employee, Ray shot him in the back."

"Didn't the police realize you hadn't done anything wrong?"

"I'd been a juvenile delinquent who'd arrived with the gunman. And even though Ray panicked and bolted from the store, leaving me to face the consequences, no one believed I wasn't a part of the robbery." He clicked his tongue. "I knew I was going down for it anyway, so I kept my mouth shut until the public defender arrived. As part of a plea bargain, I gave the cops Ray's name."

"I can't believe they didn't realize your innocence. If you'd have been guilty, you wouldn't have stuck around."

"That's what I thought. But the owner of the convenience store was a well-loved member of the community. And he was paralyzed by a bullet to the spine. Local activists had been pushing law enforcement to crack down on juvenile crime, and I was the one they cracked down on first."

"And you went to prison for a crime you didn't commit," she said, softly.

He blew out a sigh. "Five years. And during that time, my girlfriend died in a drive-by shooting and my baby went to foster care."

She scooted closer and took his hand in hers. "You've shown them all. The police. The community."

"No, I haven't shown them all. Not yet. But someday, I hope to."

Her fingers gave his hand a gentle squeeze, warming his skin, his heart, and triggering a burst of hope. He met her gaze, hoping to see that she'd taken his side and believed his story, yet expecting to hear some reason for the evening to end, some reason for him to leave.

Diana's heart went out to the one-time delinquent and ex-con, a man who was trying to make the best of a life that had started badly and only gotten worse.

She slid closer to him, her thigh nearly touching his, then slipped her arms around him and gave him a hug, offering her comfort, her support. "I admire the man you've become."

Zack wrapped his arms around her, drawing her close. His woodsy scent taunted her, tempted her.

She wasn't sure what was going on inside her heart, but it was more than sympathy, more than admiration. And it both intrigued and frightened her.

As she dropped her arms slowly, her fingers rested on his shoulders. Their eyes met, and time seemed to stop as a powerful emotion threatened to consume her. And so did an overwhelming urge to kiss him.

Her conscience urged her to take it slow, to hold back. To behave. And for a moment, she thought the good girl who lived inside of her would win out, as was usually the case.

But her lips parted of their own accord, and her fingers stroked his shoulders, slipping down to his chest.

Then, as if she had no mind of her own, she gripped the fabric of his shirt and pulled, drawing his mouth to hers.

Chapter Ten

The kiss began softly, tentatively, much as it had before. But this time, passion sparked something deep inside her.

She couldn't seem to get enough of his taste, his scent, his touch. As their tongues caressed, a shiver of heat slid through her bloodstream, causing an ache low and deep in her belly. An ache only Zack could fill.

Hands groped, touching, exploring, grasping for something to hold onto as hormones raged and desire blazed between them.

He leaned back, against the armrest, pulling her to him, with him, as he adjusted himself on the cushion and stretched out. They necked liked a couple of teenagers with a hormonal overdose.

Diana was lying on him, breasts splayed against his chest, her hips pressing against his. Rocking. Seeking. Feeling the heat, the power of his erection.

She relished being on top—in charge, but just barely.

Their breaths mingled, panting, filling the lust-charged air between them.

But Zack seemed to be holding back.

She stiffened.

Had she done it again?

Gotten too wild? Too brazen?

She drew back, breaking the kiss. Pulling away.

He didn't say a word. He merely watched her, those sky-blue eyes clouded with something—desire, she hoped. Or was it disappointment?

"I'm sorry," she said.

"About what?"

About her uncontrolled feelings. About wanting desperately to make love on the sofa, to fall onto the floor in a naked, passionate heap.

"I got a little carried away."

He sat up, brushed a strand of hair from her cheek. "Don't be sorry."

"Things are moving a little too fast," she said. Although she seemed to be the one who'd gotten carried away, who was pressing for more.

She expected him to be angry. To call her a tease,

like Travis had done. Or to come up with some other judgmental comment, like the one Peter had made the first time things had gotten out of hand between them.

But Zack didn't say anything like that.

"I think we're both skating around feelings that are a little scary," he admitted. "I don't have a problem taking things slow. I'm just glad that we're facing them head-on. So feel free to call all the shots, honey."

He was putting *her* in charge of their relationship—or whatever it was they were involved in?

She didn't know if she liked the idea of calling all the shots, but it did make her feel better about him. About them.

And about the heady feelings and emotions she was afraid to analyze.

"Would you like us to take a break from each other for a while?" he asked, his brow furrowed, his eyes glimmering with something she couldn't decipher.

"I don't think so." She raked a hand through her hair, thinking she ought to scoot farther away from him while at the same time wanting to reach out and pull him closer. "Maybe we can get together again this weekend."

"Sounds good to me. But I've got to work on Saturday. And Bob asked me to be a fifth in his monthly poker game that night. He needed someone who'd sub, and I'd hate to tell him no, after already agreeing."

"I understand. That leaves Sunday. Maybe you can go to church with us."

His eyes widened like she'd hauled off and slapped him silly. "Oh, no. I can't do that."

"Why not?"

"Several reasons. For one thing, I don't belong in a church. Heck, I always pick up my pace whenever I walk by one."

"What's the other reason?"

"Sundays belong to Emily."

She'd forgotten.

"But that doesn't mean you and the girls can't join us," he said. "I'm taking her to the zoo. Are you up for something like that?"

Taking the girls to the zoo?

It was just the kind of thing she'd like to do with him. Something slow and easy. Something that involved the kids and let them experiment with the family-type stuff. But she was a bit short on cash—again. And she had this need to pay her own way. Because her father had made such a big deal about the financial help he'd had to dole out to her and Peter, she supposed. And because she'd had to rely on him again, after Peter's death.

She would have to get over that. But she still hated to have Zack treat them to a day at the zoo. It just didn't seem right when things were so…well…so undecided between them.

"A guy at work gave me some passes," he said. "I've got enough for you and the girls to have one, too. So, what do you say?"

She brightened. "Then we'd love to go with you and Emily."

"Great. Why don't we meet by the carousel? Just let me know when."

Church got out at eleven-thirty, but she usually stood around and chatted with friends for a while. "Does noon work for you?"

"Why don't we make it twelve-fifteen, just to be on the safe side."

"All right."

He stood, then reached down and took her hand, helping her up. "I'd better let you go."

"What about the ice cream?" she asked.

"You still have to go pick up the girls, don't you?"

She nodded, amazed at his thoughtfulness, at the way his big hand gently enveloped hers, held her close. Safe.

She found herself at odds.

It would only take a phone call to Mrs. Pringle, and the girls could spend the night. But Diana couldn't do that. Not after she'd told Zack she wanted to take things easy. Not after he'd accepted her terms and seemed to respect them.

So why was she struggling with that dormant wild side of hers? In spite of a moral battle going on in her heart, she walked him to the door and told him good-night.

The good girl had won.

But it was a bittersweet victory.

And neither side was pleased.

Zack held Emily's hand as they waited next to the carousel in Balboa Park, near the world-famous San Diego Zoo, where he planned to meet Diana.

He'd lied to her the other night, when he told her he had admission passes. But once or twice before, he'd sensed her reluctance to let him pay for things. And he'd gotten that same vibe again. He wasn't sure why it was a problem for her.

The precarious relationship they'd found themselves in, maybe.

So he'd purchased all five tickets before he'd gone to get his daughter.

Usually, he didn't pick up Emily until noon, which is what he'd agreed to with the Tanners when he'd first been released from prison. At the time, he'd been content with the arrangement. But now that the adults had gotten to know each other, and Emily seemed to be adjusting to having two daddies, Zack supposed he could probably start having her for the entire day, if he wanted to.

He'd have to talk it over with Brett and Caitlin.

Emily tugged at his hand. "Are they coming soon?"

He glanced at his watch. It was just after twelve. "It shouldn't be much longer."

"Since they're still not here, can I ride the white

pony again?" Emily asked. "It's stopped going around and around."

Before he could respond, a child's happy voice called out, "Zack! Emily!"

Clapping her hands and jumping up and down, Emily cried, "They're here! Can I run and meet them?"

"Sure." He was glad the kids were eager to get together. He was, too. It had been four long days since he'd last seen Diana, since her kiss had nearly turned him inside out.

He hoped she didn't have any regrets about kissing him. She'd stopped things from going too far, but she'd also agreed to a day at the zoo, so she couldn't be feeling too remorseful.

She also seemed okay with his offer to let her control the direction their relationship would take.

Well, their relationship or whatever it was they were doing.

He was still stumbling over just what was going on between them, especially since that mind-spinning, breath-robbing romp on her sofa had convinced him that they'd left friendship in the dust.

The girls met in the middle, halfway between the adults making their way toward each other.

Zack's gaze locked on Diana's, but that didn't mean he hadn't already taken in every bit of the angelic vision moving his way. An angel wearing blue jeans, a yellow cotton blouse and a shy smile.

He figured she was feeling just as awkward, just as nervous, as he was.

"Hey." He tossed her a grin. "You're a little early."

"Well, we're pretty excited about going to the zoo." She placed a hand on each of her daughters' shoulders, but her eyes remained focused on him, her lips bearing the whisper of a grin.

Was she actually excited about seeing him again?

A glimmer in her eyes said she was.

"Come on," he said. "Let's start walking. I promised to get Emily home by six."

The girls skipped in front of them, chattering about all kinds of things, oblivious to the adults trying to keep up with them. All the while, sexual attraction swirled between him and her, stirring up desire and setting Zack's imagination on end.

He had an urge to slip an arm around Diana or to take her by the hand, but he wasn't sure how she'd feel about it.

Damn. What had compelled him to let her be in charge of things?

His fear that he'd forget who he was and where he'd come from, for one. The fact that she might come to her senses along the way and tell him it had been nice while it lasted, for another.

Okay. So he'd take one day at a time. And today, he was spending the day at the zoo, where he felt about as free as the caged animals he'd come to see.

At least when it came to pursuing the woman at his side.

* * *

The afternoon had been picture-book perfect. They'd ridden the tour bus and seen the bulk of the park, including the elephants, giraffes and kangaroos. Then they'd stopped by the nursery, where they watched through the window as a zoo employee held a diapered baby chimpanzee and fed it a bottle.

"Isn't that the sweetest thing?" Diana asked Zack.

"If you say so." He laughed, a grin dimpling his cheeks and crinkling the edge of his eyes, making him look both boyish and wise at the same time.

"I miss not having a baby to hold and rock. The girls are growing so quickly."

His eyes sparked with mischief as he looked at her daughters and asked, "And which one of the girls does that little monkey remind you of?"

"Not me!" Jessie said. "I was bald, huh Mommy?"

"Hey," Becky said. "I didn't look like a monkey, either."

"Maybe you used to eat a lot of bananas," Emily added, provoking an onset of the giggles that had become a habit that afternoon.

The girls had gotten along so well that it was hard not to wonder what it would be like to have a blended family.

"Can we go to the petting zoo before we leave?" Becky asked. "I want to feed the baby goats."

Diana placed a hand on Zack's arm in a move that seemed so natural, so parental. "Do you mind?"

"No, it sounds like fun. Let's go."

Moments later, they were inside a fenced-in area that allowed children to pet and feed various deer, goats and sheep. Zack dug through his pockets, pulling out quarters for the vending machines and helping the girls get handfuls of pellets.

Diana watched Zack, his face lit up, his expression vibrant, obviously as enthralled by the antics of the animals as the children were.

What an interesting day this had been—the kind of awe-inspiring day that made dreams seem possible, the future appear bright.

Peter, the girls' father, had spent all his free hours at church and never enjoyed activities with her or the kids. It was one of the things she'd resented about him, about their marriage.

Well, one of several.

As the girls took off, each one scurrying to pet their favorite critters, Zack sauntered toward Diana, boasting a rugged edge softened by a sexy pair of dimples she could get used to seeing.

"I think you're having more fun than the girls," she said.

"You're probably right. My grandmother brought me to the zoo once or twice when I was about Emily's age, but I can't remember it being so neat." He turned to watch the girls, his arm brushing her shoulder, warming her from the outside in. Marking her somehow, branding her.

She had the urge to slip her arm through his—just like any other mom and dad taking their kids to the zoo.

But she held back.

She was still treading softly, afraid to trust her feelings. Afraid to let go.

"Oh, no," Becky cried. "Yuck. Emily ate goat food."

"No, I didn't," the blond pixie said. A slick dirty smudge across her chin, mouth and upper lip contradicted her claim. "I just took a little lick, that's all."

"Will that hurt her?" Zack sobered and scrunched his face, as he looked at Diana. "I don't mean the goat food, but the animals have been eating out of her hands. And Caitlin is pretty careful about germs and stuff."

Diana smiled. His concern and his obvious respect for Emily's mother touched her. "I'm sure that sort of thing happens all the time. But I think a trip to the restroom to wash her face and hands is in order."

Besides, it was nearing the time to leave. So, Diana rounded up the girls and took them all into the ladies' room so they could clean up, while Zack waited for them outside.

As she lifted Emily to reach the sink, the girls continued to chatter away, but her thoughts remained on Zack, on the paternal role he'd taken on today.

She supposed a trip to the zoo, even with three pint-sized chaperones, was a little bit like going on a date.

It was weird to think of herself dating someone.

But it was also kind of nice.

Throughout the afternoon, she hadn't been able to keep herself from stealing glances at him, appreciating him—his size. His stance. The way that shank of dark hair had fallen onto his forehead. The turquoise flecks in his eyes when the sun hit them just right.

There wasn't anything about him that didn't turn her head and stir her heart.

She set Zack's daughter down on the floor, turned off the faucet, then pressed the button to start the dryer mounted on the wall. With a whirr, the warm air began to dry Emily's hands.

The little girl was as cute and sweet as could be, and it was obvious Zack adored her.

As Becky and Jessie stood in line behind Emily, their hands dripping wet, Diana's thoughts returned to the man who waited for her—for them—outside. But only for a moment.

The animation in Emily's voice drew her to the girls' conversation.

"And do you know what?" Emily asked, her eyes wide, her voice bubbling with excitement. "When I grow up, I'm going to marry Bobby Davenport."

"But he's eight years old," Jessie said, "and you're only four."

"That's okay," Emily countered. "I'm going to be five pretty soon."

"Yeah, but Bobby is *still* too old for you."

"My daddy Brett is older than my mommy,"

Emily said in her own defense. "He's twenty-nine and she's not that many."

"Hey," Becky said. "How old is your daddy Zack?"

"He's…umm…" Emily chewed at her bottom lip and scrunched her face.

Diana waited for the answer. She'd been curious about his age, guessing him to be younger than her. But she wasn't sure by how much.

"He's twenty-five," Emily said, her memory obviously coming back to her.

And Diana was thirty-two.

There was a seven-year age difference between them. Did Zack suspect that? Would it bother him to find out?

Would it make a difference?

To him?

To anyone?

She scolded herself for allowing thoughts like that to cross her mind. It seemed as though she'd been born a people pleaser.

What was wrong with going against the grain once in a while?

She rounded up the girls, then took them outside where Zack waited, leaning against the side of the building like a rebel ready to whisk her off into the sunset.

And she couldn't help but smile at the man who'd touched her heart, in spite of his youth. And in spite of the trouble he'd been in.

* * *

Zack's chest swelled, as he watched Diana herd the girls out of the bathroom.

She hadn't said jack squat about anything that had to do with her and him or the relationship that seemed determined to grow in spite of the odds. But he was beginning to feel more secure about guessing her thoughts and assuming what she was feeling.

Without a doubt, she was interested in him.

And a day at the zoo only seemed to make her even more so.

As much as he'd like to prolong their outing, to make it last into the night, he'd told Caitlin he'd have Emily home by six.

"Are you ready to go?" he asked Diana.

"Sure."

As they headed toward the main gate, his arm lifted, as if it had a mind of its own. He wanted to lay a claim on Diana and draw her close. But he quickly let his arm drop to his side.

He'd said she could call the shots.

And he'd meant it.

He just wished she would hurry up. He had the strongest urge to touch her again, to kiss her. And to finish what they'd started a few nights ago.

The walk to her car was uneventful, with the girls chattering about their favorite jungle animals, about the fun they'd had and about the yucky taste of goat food.

Apparently, following Emily's lead, Jessie had taken a lick of the pellets, too.

When they reached the old Plymouth that was parked about fifty yards from the carousel, Diana unlocked the doors and let the girls climb into the back. His daughter slid in, too.

"Can Emily go home with us?" Jessie asked. "Please?"

"Not today," Zack said. "She and her mom have plans for this evening."

Still, he let Emily sit in the back seat with Diana's girls for a while as he tried to drag out the last few minutes of their time together.

Diana shifted her weight to one foot and fiddled with the shoulder strap of her purse. "Thank you so much for including us today. We had a lot of fun."

"I'm glad you came." His hands itched to take her in his arms, but he slid them into his front pockets instead.

"I…uh…" She looked up at him with eyes filled with something, although he damn sure didn't want to step out on a limb and take a guess what.

As it was, his heart was alternating between soaring and sputtering.

"I know that your time with Emily is special," she said.

His hands tried to slide out of his pockets, but he shoved them back in. "Having you and the girls here made our day more special."

Oh, for cripes sake. Could he have come up with anything mushier than that?

"I...uh..." She tucked a strand of hair behind her ear and shifted her weight to the other foot. "I'm not very good at this stuff."

What stuff?

She nibbled on her bottom lip, then looked at him as if he could help her out.

But damned if he knew what she wasn't good at. And if he *did* know—for sure—he doubted a guy like him was any better at it than she was. Especially if it had to do with feelings. Hell, he'd been shoving his aside for years, and now, when he wished he knew which end of his heart was up, he didn't know what to do about it.

She reached for the fabric of his shirt, like she'd done the other night. Then she gave it a little tug. A nervous gesture? Or a hint for him to bend closer? To take her in his arms and kiss her senseless?

Maybe not. The girls were in the car. They might not be paying attention, but they were present just the same.

"I have a question about me calling the shots," she said.

"Yeah?"

"Does that mean I have to ask you for a good-bye kiss?"

He slid her a crooked grin. "Nope. All you gotta do is tell me you want one—or give me a reason to believe you do."

Then he bent and placed his mouth on hers, kissing her in a brief but meaningful way, a way he'd never kissed a woman before.

Slow. Steady.

And loaded with unanswered questions about unspoken promises.

It didn't last very long. Just long enough to know that their relationship had taken another scary, unexpected turn.

For the better, he hoped.

Chapter Eleven

Several nights during the week that followed, Zack, Diana and the girls had dinner together.

And each time, after the girls had disappeared into their rooms to get ready for bed, Zack and Diana ended their evening with a kiss. A kiss that no matter how brief, how sweet, how full of promise, always shook Zack to the core.

He supposed he should be content with that.

And he was.

But he'd never had to court a woman before. Never had to hold back and allow things to go along at someone else's pace. And even though that someone was Diana, his raging sex drive was pushing for more.

Still, he couldn't believe the changes in him. He'd been holding open doors, standing whenever she entered the room and sitting on the porch until late in the evening, even when there'd been a big playoff game on TV. And yet, he wouldn't have it any other way.

He was getting soft.

And liking it.

On Friday after work, he showed up at Diana's with two sacks of Chinese takeout. He also brought the girls a T-ball set, a couple of mitts and a practice net they could hit into.

Becky had mentioned wanting to play Fall Ball, a city-sponsored softball league for girls that would start soon. Diana hadn't yet agreed to let Becky play, since she was worried about how she'd get her to and from practices.

Zack figured he could help with transportation, since he was getting off work at three-thirty these days and was right by their house. But Diana apparently wasn't ready to commit to an offer like that.

Either way, he thought Becky would enjoy practicing in her backyard before the league got started.

It seemed that he and Diana had gradually become a couple. And his attraction to her continued to grow, making it difficult to ignore or control what simmered deep inside of him.

As he, Diana and the girls sat on the patio, attempting to use chopsticks and enjoying sweet and sour pork, chicken lo mein and fried rice, the ten-year-old blonde fiddled with her napkin, more than the food.

"Becky, is something bothering you?" her mother asked.

"Kind of." The girl glanced up. "I was wondering if Jessie and I could get a job or something."

"You're a little young for that. Is there something you'd like to buy?"

"Not exactly. I just want to go to camp with Allison and Brianna. It's going to be really cool. They have horses and everything." She reached into her pocket and pulled out a folded yellow flyer that showed a lot of wear. "See? The last one is next weekend. That's the one that Allison and her sister get to go to. It's only a hundred dollars, and it includes all the food and everything."

Diana took the sheet and studied it carefully, as though the camp was a real possibility. Then she bit down on her bottom lip and frowned. "I'm afraid that I can't spare two hundred dollars this week."

Zack had a feeling there weren't too many weeks when she could spare the money. She obviously tried hard to support herself and the girls, and with the cost of her sitter, he doubted there was much left over, even on payday.

But he had a savings account and some other cash put aside—some of it earmarked for a new paint job on the Camaro. He watched Diana carefully, trying to determine if it was only money holding her back.

She glanced down at the paper again. "It does look like a lot of fun."

"I could call Grandpa," Becky said. "And if I told him he didn't have to buy me a birthday present ever again, he might say okay and give us the money."

"No," Diana said. "I really don't want to ask your grandfather to help."

She seemed to be pretty stubborn when it came to providing for herself, but he'd like to make things easier on her, if she'd let him.

"I've got a great idea," Zack said. "Why don't I send the girls to camp?"

Becky gasped, eyes widening and a grin bursting across her face. "Really? That would be *so* cool."

"I can't let you do that," Diana said.

"Why not?"

Her eyes met his, and he could see her thoughts tumbling around inside. She glanced at the girls, at their plates.

"Are you two finished eating?" she asked.

They both nodded.

"Then why don't you go inside and give Zack and I a few minutes alone."

The alone time was something he always looked forward to, as much as he liked the girls. But this time, he figured there wouldn't be anything romantic going on.

He'd just gotten himself in trouble.

When the girls were gone, he leaned back in his seat, unable to completely shake the side of him that didn't take correction very well.

But he wasn't going to prolong the obvious. "Was I out of line for saying I'd pay for the camp?"

"No. It was really sweet of you."

"But?" he asked, wondering what it was that had her so uneasy about the offer.

"It's important for me to provide for the girls and not take handouts."

"I never meant it as a handout. I just want to help. And I imagine a weekend at camp would be good for them, and since I've got the cash tucked away, I'd like to pay for it. As a gift."

"I don't mean to sound ungrateful, it's just that…"

He reached across the table and placed his hand over hers. "Tell me what's bothering you so that I'll understand."

She seemed to grapple with her response, then she sat back in her seat. "When I married the girls' father, we always struggled with finances. He didn't seem to worry too much, saying that God would provide. But more often than not, it was my dad who seemed to be the one providing."

Zack figured it would be nice to have a father to lean on, someone to go to for help. A loan. Advice. Whatever.

Of course, Harry Logan had become like a dad to him. And so had his boss, Bob Adams.

So he couldn't complain.

"My father always worked hard to support my brother and me," Diana said, "sometimes taking on an extra part-time job, if necessary. So he couldn't understand why Peter's work was so important to him, especially since we were always struggling to pay one thing or another."

"Did Peter take on a second job?" Zack asked, knowing that *he* would, if his family needed the money.

"No. He was pretty busy trying to grow the congregation and raise money for a new church building. But I took in ironing and some data processing that I could do at home. But it still wasn't enough. So I approached my father for what Peter referred to as a loan, but what became a gift."

Zack figured that, as a father, he might have been a little ticked off if his daughter was the only one thinking about a second job, especially if she had a baby or two at home.

"My dad would always come through for us, but not without cursing and complaining."

"And so that's why you don't want to accept my help?" he asked.

"I guess so." She inhaled the night air, then exhaled slowly. "You don't know how badly I felt hearing him say things I agreed with."

Zack wouldn't like it if Emily married a guy who refused to take on a second job. And he understood why Diana's father had gotten ticked off about the situation. Of course, if Zack ever found himself in that position, he hoped he would handle it without cursing at his daughter.

"When I got pregnant with Jessie and couldn't work, it really put us in a crunch. More often than I liked, I had to call home and ask my dad for help. He must have expected the calls, but each time I'd have to ask anyway. And each time he'd swear and tell me that Peter ought to get a real job. Instead of worrying about building a fancy new church for a fledgling congregation, Peter ought to be setting aside money for a rainy day."

Zack kind of agreed. Churches were important, he supposed. But shouldn't a man provide for his family?

"This probably sounds terrible and disloyal to say, because Peter was a good man. But sometimes I think building that church was more Peter's idea than God's, that it was some kind of monument of his own making."

Diana's husband might have been a nice guy, but Zack didn't think much of him. A man ought to take care of his family and have his home running smooth before trying to tell other people what they should and shouldn't do and how they should live.

"When Peter died, the girls and I were left in a world of hurt, financially as well as emotionally. And I had no alternative but to go home to Texas, to my dad." She turned her hand around so that their palms and fingers touched. "Don't get me wrong. My dad isn't a bad man. He truly loves me and the girls, but he has a critical nature. And it seemed that all he could do was gripe about the fact that Peter didn't have a medical plan or life insurance."

Her husband had flat-out neglected his family, as far as Zack was concerned. But he figured that was Diana's conclusion to make. He damn sure didn't want to rag on her about it, like her father had done.

"Things began to look up when I got a job working as a bookkeeper at Buckaroo Ranch. I tried desperately to save enough money and get a place of my own before my dad browbeat Becky and Jessie, like he did to me and my brother. And when a friend from college told me about a job opening at a church in San Diego, I took it, believing I'd been provided a way out. And a way to support the girls on my own." Her eyes met his, seeking his understanding when she'd had it all along. "I have health insurance, although no dental. But I have a small life insurance policy. It makes things a little tight financially, but…"

Zack brushed his thumb along her wrist, caressing her skin, feeling her pulse beat steady and strong. "You're doing a great job raising the girls by yourself. And I understand how important it is for you to make it on your own. But what's wrong with accepting a gift from me? For the girls."

"I guess there isn't a problem with it." Her eyes met his. "Are you sure you don't mind?"

"Not at all. I'm glad I can provide them with a weekend at camp."

Her eyes glimmered with sincerity—and maybe something more. "Thanks, Zack."

He lifted her hand and brushed her knuckles with a kiss. "You're welcome."

A porch light turned on next door, and Diana straightened and drew her hand from his. "Let's go tell the girls."

Once in the living room, Diana called Becky and Jessie. Then she announced they would be going to camp.

"Cool!"

"Goodie."

As the girls eagerly wrapped their arms around Zack in two little bear hugs, he felt like someone special, rather than the rebel he really was.

Because when push came to shove, he might be happy to provide the girls a great trip, but there was a selfish motive involved, too.

He was really looking forward to having their mother to himself next weekend.

On Friday afternoon, Diana left work early and met Zack at the house. Together, they drove to downtown Bayside and parked behind the building that housed the Department of Parks and Recreation.

There, in the parking lot, an idling bus waited to take the children to Pine Valley.

"I'm going to miss you two," Diana said, giving her daughters a hug.

"But we'll be back on Sunday," Becky said. "It's only two days."

"I know."

Jessie nudged her sister. "Are you going to tell him?"

Becky nibbled on her bottom lip, then glanced down at her feet.

"Tell me what?" Zack asked.

"That she lost the ball you gave us. That she closed her eyes and swung as hard as she could. And that she didn't see where it went."

Becky looked up at Zack with regret-filled eyes. "I'm sorry."

"Don't worry about it," Zack said. "I'll look for the ball while you're gone. And if I can't find it, I'll buy you another one."

"No," Diana said. "If you can't find it, Becky will have to figure out a way to earn the money to buy a new one. That way, she'll learn to be more careful with her things."

"Okay," Zack said, winking at Becky. "But for what it's worth, my car needs to be washed."

"Cool." She glanced at the bus that had begun to fill. "Come on, Jessie. We better get going."

Moments later, as Diana fought the tears in her

eyes, the doors closed on the bus, the engine roared and the driver pulled out of the parking lot.

"Are you holding up okay?" Zack asked.

She smiled, brushing away the moisture under her eyes. "I'll be fine. A mama bird has to boot the babies out of the nest sometimes."

Zack slipped an arm around her. "Would it make you feel better if I took you out to dinner tonight?"

"On a date?"

"A *real* one," he told her. "Just you and me—if you're ready for it."

"I'm ready. What time will you pick me up?"

"Six-thirty. We have dinner reservations at The Grotto."

She'd heard a lot of nice things about that place. The Grotto was a five-star steak and seafood restaurant with an ocean view. "You already made reservations?"

He shot her a crooked grin. "I said you could call the shots. But that doesn't mean I'm not going to be prepared."

She laughed, then slipped her arm around his waist as they strode back to the Camaro, which could still use a paint job, but didn't look like it needed a wash.

In spite of her misgivings about having another man in her life, about the trouble Zack had been in, about their age difference, something felt right about this.

Three hours later, dressed in a simple black dress

she'd decided was her nicest outfit, she sat across from Zack at a candlelit table that overlooked the bay.

"Can I get you something to drink?" the maitre d' asked him. "Perhaps a bottle from our wine cellar?"

Damn. Zack had no idea what to ask for, other than one of the Merlots Harry had suggested he take to Diana's house a while back.

"Perhaps you'd like to look over our wine list," the tuxedo-clad waiter suggested.

"Please," Zack said, trying his damnedest to look like he knew what he was doing in a place like this—more for Diana's sake than his own. She deserved a night on the town. A special evening. And she didn't need him to embarrass her.

As the waiter handed him a menu that listed a ton of wines, he struggled to find one that looked familiar. But no such luck. He settled for an expensive bottle of Merlot, hoping that the price really did have something to do with the quality, not that he'd be able to tell.

A few moments later, the fancy-pants waiter poured them each a glass.

Across the room, Zack noticed an older man toasting the silver-haired woman sitting across from him. And in spite of his reluctance to do something goofy, something that would come across awkward and dumb, he lifted his goblet toward Diana.

She followed suit, as the sound of crystal sang out in a rich, heavenly tone.

"To a special lady," he said.

Her green eyes glimmered, flecks of gold sparkling in the glittering candlelight. "Thank you."

They didn't talk much, but that was okay with Zack. He was busy basking in the presence of the angel seated across from him.

And somehow, when the food arrived, he managed to pull it all off and look like he'd done this sort of thing a hundred times. The trick was in waiting until Diana chose a fork and took a bite, then following her lead. He liked the idea of coming across as polite, rather than inept.

"Zack, you have no idea how nice this is. I haven't ever been to a restaurant like this before."

"That's too bad. You deserve this and a whole lot more."

She flushed, or so he suspected in the candlelit room.

What was she doing to him?

Besides twisting his heart into a knot, she was turning him into a gentleman. At least, on the outside.

They shared a slice of cheesecake for dessert, then he paid the bill, tacking on a tip that seemed a bit outrageous. But heck, there were a lot of guys standing discreetly in the wings, ready to refill a water glass or whatever. He hoped they got to split the tip.

The ride home was pretty quiet, and he couldn't help wondering what was going on in her mind. Was she looking forward to the evening's end? Would she want to turn in early?

Or would she ask him inside for a cup of coffee or whatever?

Actually, he'd much rather prefer the *whatever*.

He pulled into her driveway, rather than parking along the curb, although he wasn't sure why. Maybe, subconsciously, it felt like he was coming home, too.

He got out of the car, then walked around and opened the door for her.

"I had a wonderful evening," she said as he reached out his hand and helped her slide from the seat.

"I'm glad." He followed her to the darkened porch and waited as she dug into her purse for the key. A streetlight down the way made it a bit easier to see.

They lingered outside for a moment, stars twinkling over head, the bulk of a fairly full moon smiling down on them.

For cripes sake, he was becoming a frigging poet whenever he was around her.

He supposed giving her a kiss wouldn't be out of line, even though she hadn't particularly indicated she wanted one. Besides, they always ended their evenings that way.

So he took her into his arms, prolonging his touch, his gaze. Then he lowered his mouth, claiming her as his own.

Diana closed her eyes, losing herself in Zack's embrace, in his kiss. With her arms wrapped around his neck, she ran her fingers through the soft, silky curls that hung along his neck.

As their tongues mated, his hands roamed over her back and caressed her derriere. She whimpered, drawing a moan from him, and the kiss deepened. Passion flared, making them desperate to caress, to taste.

She wanted him in the worst way, in the best way.

And she wanted so much more than a kiss.

A light flickered, and as she opened her eyes, she saw that Martha's front porch was lit up. It hadn't been when they'd arrived.

Uh-oh.

She placed her hands against Zack's chest, pressing gently but insistently, ending the kiss.

What if the older woman had been spying on her? Watching and waiting to see whether Zack had brought her home at a reasonable hour?

Then she scolded herself for freaking out about something like that.

Zack had been a perfect gentleman. And she was an adult, for goodness sake, able to see whoever she wanted, do whatever she wanted.

"Maybe we should take this inside," she said, her voice a bit breathless.

"Good idea."

She turned and fumbled for the keys in her purse, then fiddled with the lock, her fingers still trembling in reaction to Zack's kiss. A kiss that had been more powerful, more earth-rocking than the others they'd shared.

Or was she trembling out of fear that Martha had

caught her kissing Zack, a man the older woman had made no secret of disliking and distrusting?

Diana finally won the wrestling match with the lock and key and led Zack into the house. In the growing silence, something magical, mystical filled the air.

She lifted her arms and stepped into his embrace, back where she belonged. Where he held her captive in a swirl of desire she didn't want to escape.

Their tongues sought each other, swirling and tasting, unable to get enough. A moan formed low in Zack's throat, announcing he was hungry. On fire.

For her.

A surge of feminine pride and power took over, as her hands slid to the front of his chest and she began to unbutton his shirt.

He jerked the shirttail from his pants, then pulled her to him, his hands sliding up and down her waist before capturing her breasts. His thumbs stroked her nipples through the black cotton of her dress and the lace of her bra.

She wanted to remove her clothes, to hold Zack skin to skin. She wanted him, wanted this.

And she wanted it now.

She took hold of his hands, and he froze, as though he assumed she wanted him to stop.

"Come with me," she said, leading him into the bedroom.

* * *

Zack had told Diana she could set the pace. And set the pace she did.

She turned her back to him, pulling her hair aside so he could unzip her dress. And for the first time in his life, his fingers actually fumbled in nervousness as he undressed a woman.

But Diana wasn't just any woman. She was the lady who'd taken over his thoughts since the first day he'd met her.

She stood almost shyly before him, yet he sensed an eagerness, a need. And it had him nearly coming apart at the seams.

Did she have any idea how sexy she looked with the black lace of her bra and panties contrasting with her fair skin?

"You're so pretty, Diana. So perfect."

So much better than he deserved.

But he would take what she offered, cherishing the gift of her body.

She reached for his belt, tugging at it to get it undone. "I want you, Zack. And I don't think I need to be in charge anymore."

That's all he wanted to hear. He reached into his pocket and pulled out a foil packet. "I wasn't sure if this would happen, but I hoped it would. And I wanted to be prepared."

She smiled, her eyes hazed with passion.

Then he slipped off his pants and joined her on the bed, where they finished undressing, where he loved her with his hands, his mouth, his body.

When they were wild with need, he protected them both then hovered over her, giving her one last chance to change her mind. "Are you sure?"

If she stopped him, he didn't know what he'd do. Explode, he guessed. But he didn't want her to have any regrets, not afterward, when it was too late to turn back the clock.

She reached up, cupped his cheek gently. "I'm ready. And I want you inside me. Now."

As she shifted her hips and held onto his, guiding him, he entered her. She arched with each thrust, moving with him, taking and giving.

The world spun away, leaving only them. Only their passion, their need, and the incredible act of making love the way Mother Nature had surely intended it to be.

As they peaked, Diana gasped, then clawed into his back, crying out with a climax that sent him over the edge, too. He came in a burst of color, in a mind-soaring, eye-crossing, neck-arching orgasm, the likes of which he'd never had.

And as he lay on top of her, fully spent, he didn't dare move. Didn't dare speak. Didn't dare think.

Pretty Diana had a hold on him.

A hold that scared the liver out of him.

But he wasn't going to fight it, wasn't going to remind himself that she could do better than him. Not anymore.

They lay like that for a while, wrapped in a cocoon of awe and wonder, hearts racing.

And as they slowly pulled apart, Diana looked up at him and gasped. The regret he hadn't wanted to see crept into her eyes.

"I'm *so* sorry," she said.

"About what?"

She touched his shoulder, running her fingertips along the broken skin where her nails had dug into him. "I…guess…for getting carried away."

"Carried away?" He brushed a strand of hair from her face and kissed her brow. "Are you kidding?"

"No, I'm not kidding. I didn't mean to…"

"Diana, are you feeling guilty about this?"

"No. Not about making love. Just about…"

"About liking it so much?"

She furrowed her brow, but this time he seemed to be zeroing in on what was bothering her. "Yes, I guess so. I didn't mean to scratch you. Or to make all that noise."

"Those breathy little whimpers made my blood run hot, honey. You can scream next time, if you want to. I don't care. Heck, I feel like beating my fists against my chest, just knowing it was good for you."

"You do?"

His lips quirked in a smile, and he brushed a kiss

across the tip of her nose. "I'm going to do my best to make sure you get carried away every time we make love."

"But…I…" She let out a wobbly breath she'd been holding. "I've never done this before. Well, not like that, anyway. Peter used to…"

Zack waited to hear what she was going to say, but clearly it wasn't easy for her to share. "What did he used to do?"

"He didn't like the lights on. And he didn't like it if I…well, if I got too involved. He thought I was too wild."

"The hell you are. The only one with a problem in that relationship was your husband, Diana. He was a sanctimonious jerk. And he didn't deserve a woman like you."

She seemed to relax, to loosen up, although not quite enough. "What kind of woman am I?"

"You're beautiful, inside and out."

Diana couldn't believe her ears. No one, not Peter and not her father, had ever told her that she was pretty. Or special in any way. And although deep inside she knew she was attractive and that she was— or at least tried her best to be—a good person, it would have been nice to have someone notice.

Making love with Zack had been an eye-opening experience.

Peter used to roll over afterward, never holding her close. Never whispering words of endearment.

Zack, his arms still wrapped around her, nuzzled her neck. He didn't mention anything about being in love with her, and she wasn't sure she wanted him to. After all, she didn't trust herself to make good choices about men.

First there was that fiasco with Travis during high school. Then, when she'd met Peter in college, she chose him because he was so gentle, so mild-mannered and so different from her father. And so different from Travis, too. But in some ways, she thought he might have been too nice. Too lofty in a spiritual sense.

But still, Peter had been safe.

Once she'd gotten away from home, she'd enjoyed the freedom to date as well as the chance to exercise her sexuality. And even though Peter hadn't wanted to have sex before the wedding, Diana had pushed until he succumbed to temptation. And almost as though God shook a finger at their sin, she'd gotten pregnant with Becky.

They married, of course. But Peter always believed they'd done something wrong. And he never forgot that Diana had been the one who'd led him astray.

Zack stroked the curve of her hip. "Are you feeling better about this?"

She nodded. "I'm glad we made love."

"So am I. Do you care if I spend the night?"

No, she didn't mind at all. She loved the idea of waking in Zack's arms. "I'd like that."

He pulled her close, and she ran her hand along the corded muscles of his back.

It would be nice to have him stay in her bed until morning. But would any of her neighbors know his car had been parked in front of her house all night long?

Oh, for Pete's sake, she told herself. Get over it.

She wasn't going to feel guilty about something that felt so right. And she wasn't going to worry about what other people thought.

Not even Martha Ashton, who woke early and usually went out to get her newspaper before daybreak.

Chapter Twelve

At 6:07 in the morning, after an incredible night of marathon lovemaking, the telephone rang, jarring Diana awake.

She tried to dive for the receiver, but Zack's arm weighed her down.

"Hey, sleepyhead," she whispered.

"Huh?" He drew her even closer to his chest, her bare bottom resting comfortably in his lap.

"Zack, the phone is ringing."

He lifted his arm, allowing her to snatch the receiver from the cradle.

"Hello."

"Diana, are you okay?"

Uh-oh. It was Martha.

"I'm fine. Why?"

"Because that man's car is in your driveway. And it has been since about two this morning when I got up to go to the bathroom."

Diana dug deep into her imagination, searching for a lie. The best thing that came to mind was that Zack's car wouldn't start last night, and he had taken a cab home.

But she couldn't seem to form the words to save her soul.

"Oh," Martha said, in the short, clipped sound of a gavel.

"Is there something you need?" Diana asked the woman.

"No. I just wanted to make sure you weren't lying in a bloody heap. I guess you're all right. Sort of."

Guilt reared its head, jabbing at Diana, stirring up all kinds of insecurities she'd thought she'd outgrown.

"I'm fine, Martha. Thank you for checking."

"Well," the woman said, releasing the word in an exaggerated humph. "I don't need to tell you that I disapprove of your behavior."

Diana's chest tightened, and her stomach clenched. But she wasn't going to discuss something this special, this personal, with her neighbor. Not when she had a naked man in her bed.

And she wouldn't discuss it with Martha later, either.

It wasn't anyone's business but hers and Zack's.

"No, Martha. You don't have to tell me anything. And I don't owe you an apology or an explanation. What I do in the privacy of my home, whether it's something real or created in your imagination, is my business. I do, however, appreciate your concern."

When the line disconnected, she hung up the phone and turned to see Zack lying on his side, his upper body raised, braced by an elbow. "What was that all about?"

"My neighbor noticed your car in the driveway. And she doesn't approve of sleepovers."

"Are you okay with that?"

The call? Or the sleepover?

She definitely wasn't all right with Martha's opinion. Some things, like the need for approval, ran deep after so many years. But she managed a smile for Zack. "I'm fine. How about you?"

"I'm used to people pointing their fingers at me. But I don't like them doing it to you. What we shared was good, Diana. And it was *special.*"

She nodded, trying to take on that attitude, too. "How about a cup of coffee?"

"Sounds good."

"Why don't you take the first shower," she suggested. "I'll rustle up something for us to eat."

"Why don't we take a shower together?"

The idea had merit, but she had a fear that Martha might come charging up the steps and knock at the door. Okay, so that phone call had probably been the end of it, the one and only confrontation they'd have. But it was hard keeping her worries to herself without letting Zack think she regretted what they'd done.

Because she didn't.

It had been special. Wonderful.

But if Martha told Reverend Morton about her having a man spend the night, would he fire her for something like that?

It didn't seem likely. But then again, he was a minister. And Diana had known one particular pastor who'd been self-righteous. And, at least in Peter's case, when it came to forgiveness and turning the other cheek, a minister didn't always practice what he preached.

"That call was a little unexpected," she admitted. "So I'd really like to have a cup of coffee and think about how I should have responded, in case she mentions anything to me again."

"All right." He brushed a kiss across her brow, then climbed from bed.

His body—hard, buff, tanned and naked—taunted her, telling her that Martha could take a flying leap and that standing under the shower head with Zack sounded a heck of a lot better than a cup of coffee.

But she fought the temptation—this morning, anyway.

Should she have put up more of a fight last night?

She swore under her breath, something she hadn't done since she was a child and had mimicked her father. She'd gotten a smack that time. But she was angry and frustrated now. And another word hadn't seemed to do the trick.

After all, she hadn't done anything wrong or sinful last night. But she didn't like others thinking she had.

And *that,* more than anything, stirred up a ration of guilt.

Would she ever stop trying to please everyone but herself?

Zack stood under the pulsating spray of hot water, amazed at what he and Diana had shared last night. He'd had other lovers, but none had touched something deep inside of him, not like Diana had.

And maybe what touched him most was that she'd been wounded, too. By a father who focused on her flaws, rather than her perfection. And by a husband who didn't appreciate the angel in his arms.

But Zack would appreciate her, value her. And that made him realize he *did* have something to offer her. His respect. His desire to create a family with her and the girls. His love.

The reality of what he felt for her, what he wanted, slammed into him.

It was too early to think about a commitment like marriage, he supposed, but that's what he wanted. To have Diana, at least in some way and at some level, to know she belonged to him. To know that she had the same claim on him.

But damn. He was on parole.

Among other things, he still worried about agents from the Department of Corrections swarming into his home, tearing things up, looking for contraband that wasn't there. He'd heard about the searches that, because of his parolee status, didn't require any kind of warrant. They could enter his house or car at any time of the day or night.

If it was only him at home, he'd deal with the disturbance—cursing under his breath, of course.

But he hadn't wanted to subject Emily to something like that. And he felt the same way about Diana and the girls.

So what was he going to do? Ask her to marry him in two-and-a-half years, after his parole was up?

But asking her to marry him in the first place… He had no idea how Diana really felt about him. Or how she might someday feel.

Could she ever love him?

He hoped so, because he sure felt different in her arms—not like a rebel or a guy with a chip on his shoulder. But like some kind of hero.

After shutting off the faucet and climbing from the shower, he dried off, then put on the clothes he'd worn last night.

He'd said he'd been prepared for anything, but even though he'd hoped they would make love yesterday, he hadn't brought a change of clothes. The condoms, yes. But spare clothing and a shaving kit would have been too much.

Heck, just having them in the trunk of his car probably would have jinxed things.

He opened the medicine cabinet and pulled out a tube of toothpaste, squeezed some on his finger and made an attempt to brush his teeth. Maybe he'd end up bringing a few of his things over here for the times when he might stay the night.

Damn. He was sure making a lot of plans when they hadn't discussed their feelings or what the future might bring.

He had it bad, didn't he?

After putting the bathroom back in order, he headed out to the kitchen, where the aroma of fresh-perked coffee welcomed him.

Diana stood near the table, barefoot, wearing an old blue robe and holding a chipped yellow mug in both hands. But he didn't think she'd ever looked more desirable. She reminded him of a sleep-tousled angel, passing a little time on earth with the mortals.

"Good morning." He brushed a kiss across her brow, being careful not to jostle her cup of coffee. "It's your turn in the shower, if you're ready."

"Good. I'll make it quick." She grinned as she headed to the counter, where an empty mug waited. She filled it with the dark, rich brew, then handed it to him. "I'll fix breakfast after I get out of the shower. But in the meantime, there's orange juice in the fridge. And bread in the pantry, if you'd like some toast."

"Take your time." He tossed her a carefree smile. "I'll just go out and enjoy my coffee on the back porch."

"Good. I'll join you in a while." Then she headed for the bathroom.

Zack carried his mug outside, watching as the steam curled into the morning air.

The sun had only started its ascent in the sky, but the warmth had already dried the dew from the plants and the patio furniture.

The grass, he noticed, looked a bit long and shabby. Maybe he'd mow today.

Funny thing, when he'd been a teenager and his uncle had made him do yard work, he'd hated it. But here he was, looking forward to a day outside, to puttering around Diana's house.

Maybe he ought to go home first, change clothes and shave. Unless she wanted him to stick around a little longer this morning. He supposed he'd better play it by ear.

As he scanned the backyard, he spotted the tee he'd given Becky sitting alone and empty, which reminded him of his promise to look for the softball she'd lost.

He took a sip of coffee, then set the mug on the table and started across the lawn. When he got to the wall that bordered the construction site, he peered over the top to search.

No luck. Maybe someone had already found the ball and taken it home.

He looked over his shoulder, scanning Diana's

yard again. Maybe Becky had sent it sailing over one of the wooden fences that separated her house from the neighbor's. He strode across the lawn in his bare feet, then peered over the fence and into Martha Ashton's backyard.

The older woman was outside, bent over a rose bush, clipping yellow buds and placing them into a glass vase that sat on the sidewalk.

No ball in her yard, either. At least not that he could tell. Had it landed behind one of the many plants and shrubs?

"What are you doing?" the woman asked in a brusque tone, as she straightened and crossed her arms. "You have no business looking over that fence and snooping in my yard."

If Zack still carried a Grand Canyon-sized chip on his shoulder, like the one he used to have before Harry had worked a bit of magic on him, he might have had a surly response for the woman. As it was, he decided a polite explanation would do the trick.

"Becky and Jessie lost their ball. I was just looking for it."

She lifted her nose. "The girls went to camp yesterday afternoon. Don't try to snowball me."

He shook his head, cursing under his breath, and stepped away from both her property and the icy glare.

He'd better steer clear of that woman. With an attitude like that, she could only mean trouble.

* * *

Zack spent the night with Diana on Saturday, too. And their time together had been sweet, their love-making unbelievably good. And not once had he made her feel like anything other than a perfect lover.

Yet neither one of them had talked about the future. On Sunday morning, she'd asked him if he wanted to attend church with her. And he quickly but politely declined. She thought about staying home, too, but realized Martha would have a lot more to talk about if she did.

Zack mentioned taking Emily to the tide pools in La Jolla today and then going by to see his grandmother in the convalescent home. Diana would have enjoyed meeting the older woman, if he'd invited her to go along.

But he hadn't.

So she supposed she wouldn't see him until this evening, when he went with her to pick up the girls. The bus was due back in town at six.

Several times during the sermon and even after church, Diana noticed Martha eyeing her carefully. But to the woman's credit, she didn't appear to whisper anything to anyone else, so the morning pretty much progressed as usual.

Except that today Diana didn't feel like lingering and visiting with the others. She was eager to get home.

Feeling guilty?

Not about loving Zack, she responded to the internal voice that sounded too much like Peter.

Loving Zack.

Realization settled around her, as she faced what she'd been ignoring. She'd fallen in love with Zack.

They hadn't discussed where their relationship was going, what either of them expected or what they felt. And they really should have since there wouldn't be much of an opportunity to do so before the girls returned tonight.

Still, she climbed into her car and drove home, where she spent the afternoon doing laundry and scrubbing bathrooms, chores she'd neglected to do because she and Zack had spent the weekend in bed or curled up on the sofa watching TV.

At just after five o'clock, the doorbell rang. She assumed it was Zack, arriving early.

She placed the towel she'd been folding on top of the others, then hurried to let him in.

As she swung open the front door, expecting to see Zack's smiling face, Martha glared back at her.

The woman, whose cheeks were flushed an angry red, held a canvas moneybag in her hands.

"What's the matter?" Diana asked.

"*This* is." The woman lifted the empty bag and shook it in front of Diana's face. "The church offering was stolen. Where's that criminal who's been staying with you?"

"Now wait just one minute, Martha. What are you implying?"

"Only the obvious. I brought the weekly collection home today, like I always do, so that I could count it and deposit it in the bank on Monday morning. It was sitting on my kitchen table this afternoon, but now it's gone. *Stolen*."

"Zack didn't take it," Diana said. He couldn't have. Not the man she'd come to know. To love.

"He's a convicted felon who robbed a convenience store," Martha countered.

Diana wanted to defend him, to tell Martha he'd gone to prison for a crime he hadn't committed. But what was the use? The older woman she'd always thought of as a friend wouldn't believe it. "You've judged him guilty, just because he served time."

"Yes. *And* because I caught him looking in my backyard yesterday. He was probably casing the place, trying to find an easy way in and out of my house."

Martha had seen Zack peering into her yard? Why would he have done that? For a moment, doubt settled over her, but reason rallied.

Diana believed in Zack.

He wasn't involved in the Speedy Stop robbery. And he didn't break into Martha's home to rob her.

"I haven't called the police yet," Martha said. "But I'm going to. And as a courtesy to you, I'm advising you to talk to him. To get him to give back the money before he gets into any more trouble than he's already in."

He *would* be in trouble, Diana realized, although she didn't know how much.

He was on parole. If Martha accused him, would the police automatically lock him up? Wouldn't they need probable cause or something like that?

"I'm standing behind Zack, Martha. He couldn't have taken that money."

Martha crossed her arms and slowly shook her head. "For your sake, I hope you're right. But I'd be remiss in not telling the police about my suspicion."

Then she turned and walked away.

Diana stood frozen in the open doorway. Before she could recover or regroup, she heard the sound of a car approaching.

It was Zack.

He parked the Camaro in her driveway, climbed out and strode toward her.

A grin lit his face, but it didn't last long.

Probably because she'd found it impossible to return his smile and offer him the warm greeting he deserved.

His expression sobered. "What's the matter?"

How did she tell him about an accusation like Martha's? She certainly couldn't blurt out the news in the front yard for all the neighbors to hear. "Come inside first."

He followed her in, and she shut the door.

When she turned to face him, he gently placed his

hands on her shoulders, his eyes filled with compassion, concern.

"Martha just came over here in a huff," Diana began. "The church offering, which she'd brought home, was stolen. And she seems to think you might have taken it."

His hands slid off her shoulders, then dropped to his sides. "So that old biddy accused the only possible criminal, the known ex-con."

"I know how you feel—"

"Do you?" A flare of anger and pain filled his eyes.

No, she supposed she didn't know how he felt. Not really. She'd never been accused of a crime she didn't commit. And as far as she knew, this was the second time it had happened to Zack.

He crossed his arms. "After you left for church, I pulled some weeds in the backyard. And then around eleven-thirty, I went to get Emily. You can ask Caitlin."

"I don't have to talk to her, Zack. I believe you."

Somehow, she didn't think that was enough for him. And she didn't know what else to do or say, other than to tell him all she'd heard.

"Martha is calling the police. And she'll probably accuse you."

"That doesn't surprise me."

It didn't surprise Diana, either, since Martha had been distrustful of Zack from the start. For the most part, Martha was a good woman who wouldn't intentionally hurt anyone. But her suspicion of Zack was far from harmless.

"How will an accusation like that affect you, being on parole and all?"

He shrugged. "I'm not sure. They need some proof to arrest me. And they won't find it. I've never even stepped foot on that woman's property."

"She said you were casing out her place yesterday morning."

"Oh, for cripes sake." Zack shot her an angry, wounded look. "I was looking to see if Becky hit the ball over there. And Martha flipped out. Now I know why. She's been suspicious of me since day one."

Diana stepped forward, her arms lifting to embrace him, but he turned away, not letting her touch him or console him.

"Don't shut me out," she said.

"Why not? Don't you realize that your faith in me doesn't matter? It will only drag you down with me."

"I don't care about that."

He blew out an emotion-laden sigh, then took her in his arms, holding her close. "You have to care, Diana. You've got two sweet little girls to worry about, not just yourself."

She inhaled his scent, his strength. "But I have you to worry about, too. I love you, Zack."

He gripped her tighter, as though desperate to hang on and never let go. "You have no idea how much that means to me, but it's not enough." Then he slowly released her. "I can't stay any longer. I don't want to be here, at your house, if the police come to talk to me. I don't want you to go through that."

Then he headed for the door.

"Where are you going?"

"I've got to call my parole agent and give him a heads-up. I figure it will go easier on me if I do."

"You can use my phone."

"No, I'd rather not stick around any longer." He opened the door, and she followed him outside.

"Please don't leave, Zack. Not yet."

"I have to." He was in his car before she could stop him. "There can't be anything between us, Diana. I knew better from the start. It just won't work." Then he turned the ignition, the engine roaring in response.

"But, Zack," she said, opening her heart and soul to him. "I'm in love with you. Doesn't that mean anything to you?"

He paused for a moment. Had her words sunk in? Touched him? Was she convincing him they could be a team? Partners, friends, lovers?

He caught her gaze, but he didn't smile, didn't weaken. "I love you, too. And this is tearing me up. But it's the only way. And the quicker, the better. A relationship with you was a mistake from the get-go. And love isn't enough."

Tears welled in her eyes, and a scream of frustration strangled in her throat. How could he throw it all away like that? Her love, her faith in him.

He'd said it wasn't enough.

For years she'd tried to be good, to please her father. And then later, to please Peter. But it hadn't helped. And she refused to swallow her pride again.

She'd be damned if she'd beg and plead. If her love wasn't good enough for Zack, he didn't deserve it.

Then she turned and walked into the house, her heart broken and her spirit struggling to be whole.

The slam of her front door echoed throughout the neighborhood.

And she didn't give a damn who heard it.

Chapter Thirteen

Zack walked into his apartment and headed straight for the phone. But the first call he made wasn't to his parole agent. It was to Harry Logan.

When he told the retired detective what had happened, what he was being accused of, Harry took charge. "Just sit tight, Zack. Don't call anyone yet. I'm going to have Nick Granger check into things and run a little interference."

Zack didn't know Nick very well, just that he was a detective, Harry's son-in-law and one of Logan's Heroes. "What do you think Nick can do?"

"He can probably help rule you out before anyone down at the Department of Corrections hears anything."

"I hope you're right."

"Listen, Martha Ashton rarely leaves church until well after noon. And you were at the Tanners' house by then."

"After that, Emily and I went by Burger Bob's, and I've got a receipt. Then we went by to see my grandmother at the rest home. She'll testify to that. Other than Emily, I don't think anyone can verify that we were at the tide pools, but I'd rather not put my daughter through any questioning."

"Slow down, Zack. I know you're stressed about this, and rightly so. But let's see what Nick has to say first."

"All right."

"Are you going to be okay? Do you want me to come by?"

"I'll be fine, Harry. Thanks for going to bat for me. I sure appreciate it."

"No problem, son."

When the line disconnected, Zack held the receiver for a while, amazed that Harry would stand by him—no questions asked.

No one had ever done that for Zack before.

Except Diana. She'd offered to stick by him, even if he pulled her down, too.

She loved him.

And he'd had to walk away.

It had just about ripped out Zack's heart to see her cry, to know he'd been responsible for her pain.

But any kind of relationship with him would only bring her shame and disappointment. And the sooner she realized that, the better off she'd be.

Every time there was a theft or another crime, he'd always be the first suspect.

And as much as he loved her, as thrilled as he was to know she loved him, too, he couldn't do that to her. Couldn't put her in the position of always having to defend him. Not when a critical father and an idiot husband had made her struggle with having to defend herself, too.

So he'd done what needed to be done. He'd let her go.

It was better that way.

Now he sat in the recliner he'd bought a few months back, holding the television remote and channel surfing. But nothing seemed to catch his attention.

He just kept thinking about the agents who would toss his place apart, looking for something to tie him to the theft.

They wouldn't find it, though.

Zack had done a lot of things in his life, things he regretted, now that he was older and wiser. But he'd never taken anything that didn't belong to him. It was one of the lessons his grandmother had taught him, and it had stuck.

After he talked to Harry, he'd called Caitlin, telling her that he was going to cut his visits with Emily for a while. No need to put his little girl through anything, especially the shitty mood this mess had left him in.

The phone rang, jarring his thoughts. He had half a mind to let the answering machine pick up, but he snatched the receiver anyway. "Hello."

"Zack," a child's voice said, "it's me, Becky."

The ever-so-slight connection to Diana made his heart skip a beat. He gripped the receiver tight, the kid's call making him a bit unbalanced. "Hey. What's up?"

"Jessie and I want to know why you didn't come and pick us up from the bus, like you were supposed to. And why you aren't going to come over anymore."

Apparently, Diana had told them things were over between them.

Good.

So what was this about?

He doubted Diana had put them up to it. "Does your mom know you're calling me?"

"No. She's outside. And she won't tell us what's wrong. Her eyes are really red, like she's been crying for a hundred years. She said she wasn't sad, but I know that's a lie."

"And she *never* lies," Jessie said in the background. "Not *ever*."

Becky sniffled again.

Damn.

Couldn't Diana have explained this to them any better? Or at least shouldn't she be comforting them or something? Hell, he didn't know what adults were supposed to do when kids cried. "Why is your mom outside?"

"She's—" the child sucked in a wet, weepy gasp-like sound "—she's talking to a policeman on the front porch. She's telling him stuff about you."

"What kind of stuff?"

"She's telling him that she loves you and believes in you. That kind of stuff."

He'd told her things were over between them, told her that he didn't want to drag her and the kids down with him. And she was getting involved in his mess anyway?

Her devotion boggled his mind, pleasing him as well as frustrating the hell out of him.

When he'd left her house earlier, he'd heard the door slam. It didn't take a brain surgeon to know she was angry with him.

"So how come you made our mom cry?" Becky asked. "Sticking up for you and everything. I mean, she's a really cool person. And she loves you."

And he loved her, too. But he couldn't go over there now. Not when Harry had told him to sit tight. And not when he knew showing up at Diana's would only complicate her life.

"I'm sorry your mom is crying. But I can't do anything about that tonight."

He couldn't put her and the girls at risk.

Diana slept like hell on Sunday night, tossing and turning and missing Zack. She'd been mad at him, too. Angry at him for not believing she loved him enough to weather whatever life threw their way.

But nevertheless, she went through the motions of getting dressed for work, fixing breakfast for the girls.

Her day at the church office had been pretty routine, and when Reverend Morton left for a meeting with the interfaith council, she was alone.

As she replaced the ink cartridge on the printer, the office door swung open, and Martha entered.

Diana's stomach clenched, but she managed a smile. "Hello."

"I wanted you to know that the police dusted my house for prints. They found some that didn't belong to me."

Diana didn't respond.

"But they didn't belong to Zack, either. That nice detective, Nick Granger, came by personally to let me know."

A sense of relief fluttered over Diana. Not that she thought the prints would match, but that Martha had finally acknowledged Zack might not be guilty.

"You were right all along," Martha said. "And I'm sorry for stirring things up, for believing the worst of your friend. I really do try to give people second chances. But I worry sometimes. And I probably should stop reading the newspaper. There's so much evil in this world. And living alone, well…I…"

Diana stood, walked around her desk and gave the older woman a hug, willing herself to forgive her well-meaning friend, even if she'd jumped to conclusions that had caused severe repercussions for a man who'd been wrongfully accused of yet another crime.

A man Diana loved with all her heart.

The powdery scent of gardenia filled the air, as Martha held her close. "I'm so sorry."

"I accept your apology, Martha. But I think it needs to be directed to Zack."

The older woman nodded. "You're right. Perhaps, if he's at your house this evening, I can come over and tell him myself."

"That's a good idea. But I'm not sure if he'll be by tonight."

Or ever.

Diana's heart clenched at the realization that Zack might never come by again. His reasons for ending things between them went beyond this one false accusation.

"Well," Martha said, "I'd better go home. I'm expecting the plumber this afternoon between two and four. A pipe under the sink is leaking."

Diana placed a hand on Martha's back. "Thank you for coming to talk to me. I appreciate your friendship."

Martha nodded, then left.

A couple of hours later, when it was almost time to go home, the telephone rang.

"Good afternoon," Diana answered. "Park Avenue Community Church."

"Mom," Becky said, "I just wanted to tell you that

me and Jessie are at Mrs. Ashton's house. And you'll never guess what happened."

"What?"

"Megan's in big trouble. And I'm the hero. Kind of."

"What are you talking about?" Diana asked.

"I saw her in your bedroom going through your underwear. You know, in that drawer where you have that little pouch with money in it?"

Yes, Diana kept some cash hidden away in case of emergency. "She was in my room and going through my things?"

"Yeah. And guess what? I saw her put the money in her pocket."

Had Becky confronted her? "Then what happened?"

"I took Jessie with me and went and told Mrs. Ashton, because I thought that if Megan would steal money from us, she would probably steal money from God."

Wow. Diana sat back in her desk chair.

"And then guess what happened," Becky said.

Diana wasn't in the mood for guessing games. "Suppose you just tell me or let me speak to Martha."

"Okay, then I'll tell you," the girl said proudly. "Mrs. Ashton went to our house and asked to see what Megan had in her pockets. Megan started crying, and then Mrs. Ashton called Megan's parents."

"Did she admit to stealing the church offering, too?"

"Uh-huh. And after her mom and dad got done yelling at her, they walked her home. And when they came back, they gave Mrs. Ashton all the checks that were written to the church. But the money was already spent. So Megan's mom said they were going to make resta...resti..."

"Restitution?"

"Yeah, that's it. She's going to make Megan pay every penny of it back."

"What's Mrs. Ashton doing now?" Diana asked. "Can she come to the phone?"

"I don't think so. She's still talking to the policeman."

"Maybe you can have her call me when she's finished," Diana said.

"Okay."

"Thanks for letting me know, Becky. I'm sorry to hear that Megan would do something like that. And I'm sure her parents are heartsick over it."

Diana hung up the phone, heartsick herself.

And not at all sure what, if anything, she could do about it.

Zack had no more than gotten in from work when the telephone rang. He snatched the receiver, hoping it was Harry with news about how the investigation was going. "Hello."

"It's me."

Diana's voice slid over him like a balm, like a cool drink of water on a hot summer day, and his heart took a flying leap.

"I just wanted to let you know the money has been

recovered," she said. "And Martha realizes that she owes you an apology."

He supposed that ought to make him feel better, but the future would just bring about other suspicions, other accusations.

Still, curiosity niggled at him.

"Who stole it?" he asked.

"Megan."

The teenage girl who baby-sat for Jessie and Becky? He couldn't say that he was completely surprised.

"I'd sensed she was rebelling and acting out," Diana explained. "But I didn't realize how far she'd gone. Reverend Morton suggested family counseling. Hopefully, her parents will agree. They've been too strict with her, and that may be part of the trouble."

The line went silent, and he couldn't seem to do anything about it. He ought to thank her and let it go, he supposed. But he wasn't ready to cut the stilted conversation short.

"I thought you'd want to know," she added.

"Thanks. I appreciate you calling." Again, words failed him, as he struggled for a response. So he opted for something generic and free of the emotions tangling in his chest. "I guess that means you'll need a new sitter."

"Not really. Martha volunteered to help out until school starts in a couple of weeks."

"I'm glad things are working out for you."

"Are they?"

The silence ripped into him, tearing him to bits. But he couldn't give her what she needed. And he was afraid to even try.

"I love you, Zack. But I won't beg."

Then the line disconnected, leaving her words to echo in his heart.

He sat immobile in the recliner for a while, with the receiver still dangling in his hand. Finally, he came to his senses and hung up.

The rest of the evening was a blur. He'd fixed a TV dinner that tasted like crap. And then he'd opened a can of beer that seemed to go flat with each swig he took. He'd turned on the TV hoping to find a mental distraction, but there wasn't a damn thing that interested him.

All he could think about was Diana—her smile, her laugh.

Her hope.

She seemed to believe that love was enough.

But was it?

Several hours later, Zack stood on Diana's darkened front porch and rang the bell.

He ought to feel guilty coming here at this hour, waking her after midnight.

But he didn't.

As far as he could see, there hadn't been any way

around a nighttime visit. He knew because he'd tried to talk himself out of it for the past hour.

Diana peered through the peephole before opening the door, her body blocking the threshold.

She wore her faded blue robe and a somber expression that turned his heart on end. Becky had been right about her eyes. They looked like hell.

And he was the one to blame.

There didn't seem to be an easy way through this, other than to stumble and fumble and lay open his heart.

"I hope it's not too late," he said. "But I need to talk to you, and it couldn't wait until morning."

"Sure," she said, letting him in.

She didn't offer him a seat, and he didn't take one. He figured he was too fidgety, too eager to get things off his chest and out in the open.

"I'm having second thoughts," he told her. "About love not being enough."

Something flickered in her eyes, yet she didn't speak, didn't help him wade through the emotions he'd been dealing with all evening.

"So the choice is yours," he told her.

"What choice is that, Zack?"

He shrugged, thinking it should have been as obvious to her as it was to him. "Deciding whether or not you want to take a gamble on me and try to make a life together. A home."

She crossed her arms. "You don't understand. I

don't have a choice at all. My love won't allow me to step aside or turn my back on you—no matter what the future brings."

He was amazed at her unconditional support. Flattered by it. Relieved, yet overwhelmed.

Damn. His feelings were bouncing and ricocheting around his chest like a couple of chrome balls in a pinball machine.

"I won't let you down," he told her, "but just the thought of dragging you through the muck and mire of my past makes my gut knot up. I wish there was a way to protect you from it."

"Maybe I don't want to be protected. Not if it means facing the future without you."

His heart took a final tumble right there and then. Nothing meant more to him than this woman's love, than her faith in him, her willingness to stand by him no matter what.

"I love you, Diana. And I'll be happy to wait until my parole is over to marry you. You can call the shots."

She reached up, cupped his bristled cheek with her hand. "No way. I don't want to wait any longer than we have to. And as for calling the shots, we'll have to figure out a way to compromise, like other husbands and wives."

Zack's heart damn near burst out of his chest, and he took her in his arms, drawing her close, savoring the homey blend of floral-scented bath soap and the hint of fabric softener in her freshly laundered robe.

"What did I ever do to deserve you?" he asked.

"You took a chance on love. And on *us*."

Then she slipped her arms around his neck, tiptoeing and drawing his mouth to hers, sealing their love with a kiss.

But this one was different from the rest. And not because it held the hint of peppermint-flavored toothpaste.

This kiss was strong and bold, full of vows and promises, each one singing of faith, hope and love.

The world lay before them, and nothing could stand in their way.

Diana was the one to end the kiss, blessing him with a pretty smile. "Come on. Let's go to bed."

"What about the girls?" he asked. "Should we set the alarm so that I can get out of here before they wake up?"

"In the morning, we can tell them that you're going to be my husband and their new daddy. And that you'll be with us every morning and every night from now on."

He took the hand of the woman he loved and led her to the bedroom. There, he slowly began to undress her, allowing her to do the same to him.

The clock on the bureau told them they had hours before dawn and all the time in the world.

He loved her the only way he knew how—with everything he had, his body, heart and soul.

Their joining brought on a star-spinning climax

that caused them both to cry out, proclaiming their love for each other.

Once upon a time, Zack's life had been filled with one disappointment after another. But now?

How could one man be so lucky?

He glanced down at the woman in his arms, as they lay amidst tangled sheets, and pressed a kiss upon her brow.

Diana's love had offered him something he never thought was possible.

A one-way trip to heaven and a happy ever after.

And boy, was he going to enjoy the ride.

* * * * *

Don't miss Judy Duarte's next novel
A BRIDE FOR A BLUE-RIBBON COWBOY
Silhouette Romance #1776
Available July 2005

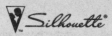
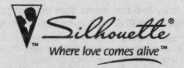

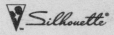

SPECIAL EDITION™

presents a new six-book continuity

MOST LIKELY TO...

Eleven students. One reunion.
And a secret that will change everyone's lives.

On sale July 2005

THE HOMECOMING HERO RETURNS

(SE #1694)

by bestselling author

Joan Elliott Pickart

Former college jock David Westport was convinced he had it all—a beautiful wife, two wonderful kids and a good business in his North End neighborhood. Sandra Westport loved her husband dearly but was positive that he did have one regret—letting her sudden pregnancy derail his chances at a pro baseball career ten years ago. And when a college professor revealed a secret that threw all the good in David's life into shadow, Sandra feared her marriage was over. Could David rebuild his shattered dreams without losing the love of his life?

Don't miss this emotional story—only from Silhouette Books.

Where love comes alive™

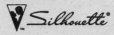

·SPECIAL EDITION™

is proud to present a dynamic new voice in romance, Jessica Bird, with the first of her Moorehouse family trilogy.

BEAUTY AND THE BLACK SHEEP

Available July 2005

The force of those eyes hit Frankie Moorehouse like a gust of wind. But she quickly reminded herself that she had dinner to get ready, a staff (such as it was) to motivate, a busines to run. She didn't have the luxury of staring into a stranger's face.

Although, jeez, what a face it was.

And wasn't it just her luck that *he* was the chef her restaurant desperately needed, and he was staying the summer....

Where love comes alive™

Coming this July from NEXT™

Sometimes a woman has to make her own luck.
Find out how Kasey does exactly that!

LUCKY by Jennifer Greene

Don't miss the moving new novel by *USA TODAY* bestselling author Jennifer Greene.